# CLYDE & DIOR

## THE RICHEST LOVE

MZ.EBONII .S

Written by Mz. EbonII.S

# DISCLAIMER

This book is intended for an adult audience due to strong language and steamy sexual situations. You have been warned.

## ACKNOWLEDGMENTS

Thanks to my mom for not killing me when I would wake her up at four in the morning with questions and ideas for this book.

Atevia, thank you for helping me when I needed it and for having patience with me when I seemed a little demanding. You have helped me with this book in so many ways. This book would not have been done so soon if it wasn't for your help and guidance.

## 1

# DIOR GIBSON

~

*GW hen you a gon' learn, learn, learn, learn, learn, learn Me na care if me tired, tired, tired, tired, tired, tired Join me I deserved it No time to have you lurking If I got right then you might like it You know I dealt with you the nicest Nobody touch me, in the righteous.*

Dior danced to Rihanna *Work* as she got ready for her night out with her girlfriends. She was too excited about going out; it'd been a good minute since she'd been out to any club with any of her friends. Adding the last curl to her hair, she blew kisses at herself in the mirror and walked out of the bathroom. Going into her large walk-in closet, she scanned her many outfits for the perfect fit for the night. Most of the outfits still had tags. One thing she loved to do on the weekend or any day was blow her man's money. Dior just recently spent five stacks on outfits she probably would never wear. Eventually, she decided on the perfect fit; she unwrapped the towel that was snugged around her curvaceous body allowing it to land around her freshly done toes. She slipped on this army-green, sexy cut out sheer bodycon dress, walking over to the other side of the closet where all her shoes were neatly placed trying to decide on which pair of heels she wanted to wear that night. After five minutes of trying to decide, she finally settled on a pair of black spiked Red Bottoms. Finishing up her outfit, her phone dinged, alerting her of a text message.

*British: Girl, you ready?*

*Dior: Yes bish, I'm just about to walk out the house.*

*British: Hurry the fuck up, everybody is already here. We're waiting on you.*

Tossing her phone on the bed without even replying back, she put on some Miss Dior perfume behind each ear and down the middle of her D breasts before walking out of the bedroom. Not knowing where Clyde was, she quickly made her way down the stairs before he stopped her.

"Where you goin'?" Clyde questioned her, stopping Dior in her tracks.

"It's British's birthday today; she wanted her girls to get together and have some sorta birthday bash at this club tonight."

"And you wearin' that?"

"Yea, what's wrong with it?"

"What you mean what's wrong with it? It's short as hell, and your breasts are hanging out."

"Ugh, Clyde, please don't start this shit tonight. The girls are waiting for me; I told them I was on my way, so I need to go. I'll be home later tonight, okay?" She sashayed over to him and kissed him on the lips. Before she could pull away, he roughly grabbed her by the waist, taking his hand and running them up her dress. Standing just inches from the front door, he pressed her up against the glass door ripping her lace thong and throwing them to the side. He forced her to spread her legs sliding his index finger between them and began to massage her clit and nibbling on her neck, grabbing her by the hair, intentionally messing up her pretty curls. Dior was furious with Clyde; she wanted so badly to pull away from him, but the way her body reacted to his touch made her vulnerable, her body submitted to every demand he made without speaking. After her second orgasm, she gathered herself and pushed him off her and hurried upstairs to the bedroom. She looked herself in the mirror, a tear streamed down her face; it wasn't a tear of sadness--she was far from sad. She was angry with herself for falling for his shit once again. This wasn't the first or third time that he did shit like that out of the four years that they'd been together; he always seemed to get his way.

    She always thought it was because of their large age gap

that he felt he had some sense of control over her. Tons of people had always asked Dior what she saw in a man that was twenty-two-years older than she was, and her answer had always been the same, *love has no color, and no age.* Fixing herself up for the second time, she went back downstairs, grabbed her purse and keys, and headed out. She slid into her Benz, started up the engine, and burned rubber. Glimpsing at the time on her Michael Kors rose gold watch, she realized that she was almost an hour late. Dior just knew British was going to be pissed at her. Finally, making it to her house, she parked her car in the driveway. Before she could get out of the car, her phone dinged informing her of a text. Checking the message, it was from Clyde, asking her where she was. Rolling her eyes, she didn't bother to respond. She shut off her phone and shoved it into her purse and headed towards the door, but before she could knock, it swung open.

"Bitch, what the fuck, you're an hour fucking late, man," a tipsy British said walking back to the living room where the other girls were. From the looks of things, they already had gotten the party started; the music was blasting, and empty Vodka and Hennessey bottles were lying around.

"Shit I thought you weren't gonna show up tonight," one of the other girls said, pouring herself a drink.

"I'm here now, so let's head the fuck out!" Dior shouted over the loud music adding another layer of lip-gloss to her plump lips and fixing her hair in the mirror hanging in the hall.

"Let's go, girls!" British shouted as she grabbed her bottle of champagne that was chilling in a bucket of ice and headed out the door. There was a party bus outside waiting on the ladies; Dior climbed inside the bus, and the other women followed behind her. All four women hooted and hollered in excitement when they noticed it was stacked with liquor and a pole in the middle of the bus. They wasted no time in pouring themselves more shots. By the time they arrived at the club, they were either good and drunk or tipsy.

As the driver parked, they all lined up to step off the bus. Dior looked around and noticed how packed the club was already--it was one of the most popular clubs in the Black and Latino community of L.A. The lines were long so long it began to curve around the building. Luckily, British was very familiar with the owner, so the bouncers nodded his head, stepped aside, and let the ladies in. Stepping inside, the club was banging--bitches were twerking, and niggas were taking shots to the head while trying to get them a fuck for the night.

The ladies made their way up to the VIP area where bottles of Patron, Henny, and a bottle of Ace of Spades champagne waited on them. British darted directly over to the liquor and began pouring herself and the girls a shot, while Dior was in her zone grooving to the music. She was a lightweight, so a couple of glasses of champagne and three shots of Henny had her feeling herself.

"Let's go dance!" Dior shouted in British's ear taking her by the hand and dragging her to the dance floor before she could answer. They stood in the middle of the dance floor, and Dior and British began to dance, rubbing up against each other. A Nicki Minaj song boomed through the club, and British was a huge fan of Nicki Minaj; she tried to live the same high-class, upscale lifestyle as Nicki, just without the singing career, but instead, she settled for a couple of sugar daddies here and there that could support the lifestyle that she wanted.

"Damn, you look good," a deep and sexy voice said in

Dior's ear. Without turning around to see who it was all up on her, she started grinding up on the guy allowing him to grab a hand full of her ass. As she continued to grind up against him, her eyes widened as she felt his dick growing; liquor turned her into a completely different woman. While enjoying herself, she felt another pair of hands wrapping around her waist and pulling her away. She looked up into the person's eyes and realized they were Clyde's hands that pulled her away from the fun.

"What are you doing here?" Drunken Dior questioned, slurring her words.

"I've been calling you, and you haven't picked up your phone," he replied calmly, eyeing the man that had his hands on his woman.

"I know, I cut my phone off, I didn't want to be bothered. I told you where I was going tonight, so there was no need to keep checking in like I'm some child." A drunken Dior spat, pushing herself away from his grasp. "I'm not going home. I'm here to have a good time with my girls tonight, so you can either stand there looking stupid, or take your ass home," Dior said turning to walk away, but he forcefully grabbed her by the arm and pulled her into him.

"Unless you want me to shoot this fucking place up tonight and dismember your fucking boyfriend over there, I would suggest you come home with me," he said calmly into her ear.

It wasn't the threat that frightened her but his calm demeanor. Dior stood there for a moment looking in his light-blue eyes; she had a sense that he was being extremely serious. Taking a deep breath, she yanked her arm from his grip, turned on her heels and began to look for British to tell her she had to leave. Clyde stood there watching the two women as they exchanged words; he didn't know what was being said, but he knew just from British's expression she wasn't too happy. Deep down, he didn't like his woman hanging out with a foul creature such as British; he knew her type all to well. She was a succubus, a demon that took the form of a beautiful woman just to suck the soul from any man. If he believed in the supernatural, he would defiantly put her in the category.

"Mmm! Daddy, you wanna come home with me tonight?" a strange looking woman asked as she began to rub herself up against him like a bitch in heat. His eyes darted to the short, five-foot-four woman. She was short and skinny, and that alone turned him off. She looked to be Latino with a horrible dye job and smelled like cheap perfume. He was disgusted by her antics, pushing her away letting her know that he wasn't interested, but like a fly on shit, she just came back. Not in the mood, he took a deep sigh, grabbed a handful of the blonde hair, and yanked it hard enough where her body bent backward like the girl from the movie *Last Exorcism*.

"Let go of me!" the woman pleaded."

But Clyde wasn't listening to her cries; he continued to hold his firm grip to where it felt as if her scalp was going to peel back. He stared at her while she looked into his wild eyes. He eventually loosened his grip to where she was able to break free.

"Fuck you!" she shouted, staggering trying to catch her balance in her five-inch heels, running her hands through her long, blonde locks.

"What did you just do to that woman?" Dior questioned, nudging him to get his attention.

"Let's go," he said, grabbing her by the arm to escort her out the club.

Once they both got into the car, Dior scooted herself to where she was almost sitting on the door, with her hands in her lap and legs crossed, daring for him to touch her. Clyde didn't care about her being upset, he had her in his presence now, and that's all that mattered to him.

"I don't want you hanging out with that British anymore."

"Excuse me?" Dior quickly turned her head towards him.

"You heard me, a woman such as yourself shouldn't be hanging with someone like her."

"Someone like her? And what the hell is that supposed to mean. She's the only friend that I have, and she's the one that's been around when you were gone on "business" trips for two to three days. An, ad you want me to just up and stop talking to her, fuck all that.

"You know what I mean, and unless you are as dumb as she is, then I expect you to fully comprehend and do as I say."

"Do as you say? I'm not your fucking puppet to fucking control, Clyde. I don't fucking know who the fuck you think I am, but I can assure you that I'm not the fucking one." She hissed, angrily crossing her arms over her breasts and going back to looking out the window.

"No, you are not my puppet, but you are my woman, and my woman will do as she's told."

"Then maybe it's time for us to go our separate ways." Dior spat back; the rest of the ride home, there were no words spoken. Once they arrived at the house, Dior hurried out of the car before he could even turn the engine off. She storms up the stairs to the front door, unlocked the door, and slammed it shut hard enough where the glass door almost shattered.

As she walked up the stairs to the bedroom to pack her things, she called British to see if she was still at the club, but there was no answer, so she just left a message letting her know she got into another fight with Clyde, and she was finally leaving him and needed a place to stay.

"You're not going anywhere, Dior," Clyde calmly stated as he stood in the doorway of their bedroom watching her walk back and forth packing her belongings.

"Why, because you said so? I love you, Clyde, I really do, but you're driving me fucking crazy. It's not just the smothering, it's you staying gone all night sometimes for two to three days at a time. You claim you're out on business trips, but I know better than that. I don't know what you're doing or whom you're fucking, but I'm not going to put up with the shit anymore. I'm tired; I need time to think...to breathe."

Once she finished stuffing her things into her bag, she picked it up and started to head for the bedroom door. Clyde stood there for a moment blocking her from leaving. She looked up at him into his expressionless face. After a few seconds, he finally stepped to the side allowing her to walk out the bedroom. Before she could make her way down the steps, he leapt over towards her, grabbing her by her hair and pushing her up against the hall wall. She was now pinned between him and the wall. She took in his aroma and couldn't help but to think how good he smelled with his hard body against hers. Her body began to react to his; her nipples started to get erect, and her girl parts began to tingle. *Stay focused, Dior. You're pissed off at him; don't get distracted*, she thought to herself.

"What the hell are you doing, Clyde? Let me go!" Dior shouted trying to push him off her, but his masculine body wouldn't budge. Examining his facial expression, she could finally see how furious he was; his jaws were clenched tightly, and his beautiful, ocean-blue eyes were now a dark-storm blue. Whenever he was feeling some kind of emotion, whether it was good or bad, his eyes would change. Either lighter blue or dark blue, but she didn't give a fuck how upset he was. She marveled in his misery; it served him right. Maybe next time he would think before he decided to be so controlling.

"Oh, mi amour, *(my love),* there's so much that you don't understand."

"Then make me understand, because clearly, I don't understand why you continue to shut me out of your life. The whole four years we've been together, you've done nothing but shut me out, and I'm sick of it. Maybe you should find you someone your own age, someone that is willing to sit around the house and wait for you to come home, because clearly, I'm not the one. Now, let me the fuck go so I can leave."

Before letting her loose, he placed his lips on hers and gave her a deep, passionate kiss, sliding his tongue into her, and she welcomed it.

"Tu m'appartiens," *(You belong to me,)* he whispered in her ear before letting her loose. She rushed over to her bags, grabbed his car keys, and rushed out the door without looking back.

## 2

## DIOR

*D*ior parked her car in front of British's house, waiting for her friend to return home from the club. British and Dior had been good friends since the first day Dior moved to Los Angeles. Dior didn't know anyone nor did she know the best hot spots of L.A until she met British in the apartment complex she was staying in, and since that day, they'd been stuck at the hip--something Clyde wasn't too fond of. Dior glanced at her phone to check the time; it was ten minutes till three. She knew she would be returning home soon, or she hoped anyway. While sitting in the car, her mind drifted off to Clyde and the first day she met him.

*Dior moved to Los Angeles a year after she graduated from high school. She was tired of being Dajah's baby sister and always being babied by Eleanor, her mother. At eighteen, her mother still saw her as Pickle, the nickname she had been given as a baby. She felt it was time for her to get out of her mom's house and get out on her own, go to college to get her MA in business, and get her alcohol license in Los Angeles--those were her main focuses, her goals.*

*Every morning, she ate her breakfast and spent an hour on video chat with Eleanor. This day was of course, no different. Once she had gotten off the phone with her mother, she decided to go out to the beach and get some much-needed vitamin d, along with a couple of drinks while she watched the sexy men of L.A pass her by. The first thing she bought when arriving to Los Angeles was a two-piece, high-waist bathing suit. Never owning a two-piece before, she was too excited to wear it out.*

*Whenever there was a family trip, her sister would say how fat she was and how ugly she would look in one with her fat stomach and big ass, so instead, she ended up wearing a pair of basketball shorts and a tank top, but now, fuck her! She wasn't around to tell her shit, Dior was at the age now where she didn't care what nobody said or felt about her body. She knew she looked good in whatever she wore. Admiring her figure in the full lengh mirror, she smiled at herself. She was thick in all the right places; she loved her body, even if her sister was right about a man not wanting a fat woman, she loved it, and that was all that matttered to her. Her mom would always say a real man would look at her and love every itch of her body no matter how small or big she was. With thick thighs that rubbed together when she walked, wide hips and a small waist with a slight pudge in the stomach area and a round ass to finish everything off, it wasn't big nor small--just enough for her man to grab onto it, whenever she got one. The last guy that Dior was involved with ended badly. Her sister, Dajah always seemed to get in the middle of her relationships. Whenever she got a good man and the relaionship was going good, suddenly, the guy ended up disappearing, never letting her kow the reason why he was leaving her.*

*After slipping on the two-piece, she tied her hair up into a high bun allowing some of her hair to fall in her face. After she was done getting dressed, she grabbed her large hobo bag and black, lace floral cover up, and she was ready to head out. Locking* the door behind her, she headed towards her 2000 Toyota black truck her mother bought her for her graduation present. Making it to the beach, she parked her truck and got out with her tote and other things in hand. As she made her way towards the beach, Dior was in awe by how beautiful the water was, it was a perfect blue--none of that dirty brown water like the Corpus Christi beach. The sand felt like piles of small cubs hugging and cuddling her small feet. She looked around for a spot to lay her towel and things down. It was still pretty early and was already crowded. Walking through the people, she stopped once she got to the perfect spot to place her things down. She was away from the crowd but not too far away where it seemed like she was being anti social. Dior began to set up. Not having any experience in putting up a beach umbrella, she found herself struggling. She looked around making sure that no one was paying attention to her. After ten minutes, she finally had the umbrella up, feeling like she accomplished something great. Her excitement was short lived when a strong burst of wind began to blow, blowing all her shit down. Dior reached over attempting to catch it, but she tripped over her tote bag landing head first in the sand. She was now covered in sand; her perfect day had now turned into a complete mess.

"Are you okay? Do you need help?" A husky, stern voice echoed through her like a empty cave. She looked over her shoulder and was hypnotized by this disturbingly attractive man that stood behind her. His perfectly tanned skin was glistening in the sun. He was so masculine with muscle on top of muscle. Thinking she finally caught her balance, she slowly tried to lift herself up to only slip and fall again. Feeling completely embarrassed, she could only imagine what he was thinking. Dior was sure he thought she was a fat, clumsy woman that should not be on the beach, but he was thinking everything but that. He reached down, wrapped his large arms around her waist, and *lifted her full-figured body frame up like she weighed nothing; she just knew her ass was heavy. While she was straightening up, she heard a ripping sound. Looking down, she saw that it was her beautiful cover up.*

*"Ugh! That's just freaking great." She pouted, taking her cover up off, folding it and throwing it beside her bag.*

*"I'll buy you another one," he said nonchalantly.*

*"Mmhm," was all that came out of her mouth. What the fuck, Dior? You can do better than that, damn. She scolded herself. Realizing that she was still in his arms, she quickly removed herself from his embrace. She saw his eyes lingering, taking in her body.*

*"Very nice," he said just above a whisper.*

*"Excuse me?"*

*"Are you okay?"*

*"Yes. I'm fine, thank you, I can be a little clumsy sometimes," she answered with a snicker, brushing herself trying to get the sand from between her thighs. The one thing she hated about sand was the difficulty of taking it off. He saw the struggle and began to help in trying to dust the sand off. Dusting Dior off, he ran his hands down her thighs then up between them barley grazing her lady parts. Quickly stepping away from his touch, there was this strong radiance that kept pulling her towards him.*

"Girl, what are you doing here?" a drunk British asked, knocking Dior out of her thoughts.

"I got into a fight with Clyde, I need a place to stay for a while until I can find a place to stay."

"Girl, you know I got you, come on." British struggled to get her key into the door, so Dior took it and unlocked the front door.

"I don't know what the fuck I'm gonna do, Brit, how the hell am I gonna find a spot to stay and I ain't got no fuckin' job?"

"Girl, I'm too drunk for this deep conversation. How about you sleep on it and we'll talk about it in the morning." British slurred as she passed out on the sofa with her clothes and heels still on. Dior took British's heels off and took the throw that was on her sofa to cover her up.

It'd been a month now, and Dior was still living with British. Although she loved her girl to death, living with her was almost impossible. Dior and British were two different type of people all together. While Dior was more laid back and quiet, British was more of an outgoing, party girl that loved to have shit going on at her spot every day. The first day that Dior was at her house, there were so many men going in and out, laid up on the sofa rolling blunts, and talking shit. That alone made Dior want to put aside her childish ways and go back to Clyde, but instead, she stayed and hit the streets in search of a job. That night Dior moved in with British, Clyde had Tony drive him to British's house to pick up his car; she threw his keys at him and locked the door--she knew she was being extra, but she didn't give a fuck. She was tired of his bullshit.

"What we doin' today, girl?" British asked walking out into the living room in nothing but a thong."

"I don't know, but I sure do wish you would put some clothes on. I don't want to see your tittes swangin' around and shit," Dior said with a laugh.

"Bitch, this my house I can walk around here butt ass naked if I felt like it." British harshly stated. Dior wasn't in the mood to get into it with her so instead she got up and left out the house sitting on the porch with her phone she fills out a couple of applications. As she filled out her second application her phone dings alerting her of a text message.

*11a.m Clyde: We need to talk.*

Ignoring the text, she continued to fill out applications.

*11:10 a.m Clyde: I understand you don't want to talk to me right now, but I don't want you staying with that woman. Tony should be pulling up any moment now to give you some money to get you on your feet.*

As she read the text message, Tony was pulling up. Dior got up from the porch and walked over to where Tony was parked

"Hello, Ms Dior," Tony greeted her with a warm smile.

"Hello, Tony, how are you today?"

"Oh, I'm hanging in there," he replied as he handed her a brown envelope

"Thank you!" she said stepping back on the curb to watch him drive off. Any other time she wouldn't accept anything from him, but the living situation she was in wasn't going to work for her; she needed to be out asap. Looking inside the envelope, there were eight bands which would be more than enough for her to get her own spot and furniture. She knew she wasn't going to be able to buy herself anything nice, but she would be satisfied with anywhere other than where she was staying. Going inside, she went into the kitchen to make her breakfast sitting the envelope on the counter to crack her some eggs. British walked into the kitchen with a robe wrapped around her body. Seeing the envelope on the counter, she picked it up and peeked inside.

"Where this come from?"

"Clyde sent it for me so I can get a place," Dior replied as she tried to snatch the envelope out of her hand.

"Shit, you might as well stay with the nigga, since he's still taking care of you. What's the point of being broken up when a nigga still givin' you money. If you don't want him taking care of you or being controlling, then you really shouldn't accept this money. Don't you think this is his way of keeping control over you?" British said as she put the money back in the envelope making her way over to the fridge to get her something to drink. After breakfast, Dior went into the bathroom to do her bathroom routine. Once she was finished and had gotten dressed, she grabbed her purse and keys and left out in search of an apartment.

# BRITISH

"*When Dior first moved to L.A, we were glued to the hip; nobody could tell us shit. We were what you would call club rats always hitting the club and romancing the streets looking for shit to get into, but ever since she got in a relationship with her nigga, Clyde, she suddenly didn't have time for me. I mean, don't get me wrong, I understand that when you got a nigga shit changes and you stop hanging out with your friends, but damn, she just completely forgot about a bitch.*" British vented over the phone to one of her many girlfriends as she rolled a blunt.

"*So, if you feel that way then, why you continue to have her in your life? Dump that bitch on the curb and go about your business, she ain't your responsibility,*" her friend stated

"*Girl, I don't know, I guess because I feel like she's my charity case. You know she ain't got nobody here in L.A but me and that foul nigga of hers. Did I tell you that she left him last night?*"

"*Girl naw, you ain't said nothin' about that.*"

"*Bitch yes, he went to the club and picked her up. He didn't want her hanging with us, so he went and snatched her ass up* and took her home. They ended up gettin' into a fight. and she left his creepy ass".

"Where she at now?"

"Bitch, she's over here at my house."

"Girl, I cant."

"Yes, now she's out somewhere lookin' for an apartment; he gave her some money for her own place."

"If he's supporting her, why they even broke up? Shit, I know when I left my nigga, he wasn't sendin' me shit, and I didn't want shit from him."

"That's the same shit I said, bitch, especially when you always talkin' about how controlling he is. I wouldn't be accepting shit from my controlling boyfriend 'cause I know he's gonna want somethin' in return in the long run. Bitch, I can't with her anymore," British said with a laugh.

After the phone conversation British was having with her friend, she went into the kitchen to get her a beer and sit and enjoy her blunt. While flipping through the channels, the doorbell rang. Taking another hit of her blunt before answering the door, she swung it open without asking whom it was, and to her surprise, it was Clyde standing there expressionless.

"Can I help you, or are you just gonna stand there all creepy and shit?"

"Where's Dior?" he asked in a deep, husky tone.

"Shit, I don't know. I don't keep tabs on her like you do, but shit, if you lookin' for some company, I can provide that for you," British seductively said as she untied her robe and opened it just enough where her breasts were showing. Clyde stood there for a moment looking her up and down, turned, and walked away.

"Creepy, old fucking man, no wonder she left your old ass." British sassed, shutting the door. She had a slight crush on Clyde with the way he carried himself as if he owned the world. That shit turned her on, and not to mention he was filthy rich. She couldn't quite understand what he saw in that girl, Dior; she was so simple, soft spoken, and just basic. British knew that he needed a woman on his arm that made him look powerful. Dior made him look everything but that.

## CLYDE NIGHT

*G*lancing at his Louis Moniet Rainforest watch, which he won at an auction last summer for twenty-five million, he saw it was nine past ten. Sitting in the same spot for the past two hours listening to his business partners go back and forth about a deal that he had already taken care of, all he could think about was Dior, and how much he needed her in his life. When he was away from Dior, a storm inside of him built up, trying to claw its way out, but as soon as his eyes were upon her, the storm dissipated. Before her, he could admit, that he was and still is a hard man to get along with. His world had always revolved around his business; at twenty, he started the Night Real Estate Corporation.

Having a father that instilled the business value in him, and also being raised by a father that wasn't the most nurturing parent, made him the man that he is now. Clyde continuously displeased his father with the life choices that he made for himself. His father would always say how much he reminded him of his mother, and that alone gave Clyde grief. As a child, he still felt that it was his fault for his mother's death since she died giving birth to him. His father always pushed him to be better than what he was. No matter how hard Clyde tried to please his father, it seemed his father was never happy. After the death of his father, he made a promise, a promise that he swore to always keep. At forty, Night Corporations was now worth four point seven billion. Owning casinos, condos, strip clubs, and hotels all over the states, and soon, outside of the states.

"Clyde, are you listening? As you know, the deal alone is worth one hundred million. It will open up so many more doors for us." The employees and partners of Night Real Estate Corp had spent many months trying to close a deal in New York. If the deal went as planned, the company would be teaming up with one of the most successful hotels which would allow them to build a hotel and casino complex.

"Yes, I am listening, and I will take care of everything," he responded to his business partners.

"Good, we will see you tonight, right?" one of the men asked.

"Tonight, what's tonight?" he confusingly asked. He couldn't for the life of him figure out what he was talking about.

"Tonight is the night of the annual harvest. I hope to see you there."

"Oh, right, yea, I'm sorry--my mind is all over the place. Yes, I will be there," he responded.

"Good, we will see you there then," the man said as they all got up and left out the office. After they left, Clyde stayed behind for the next hour signing papers. He looked at his watch and realized it was getting late. Returning his documents to the desk drawer, he left out his office, quickly reaching his Audi R8. Sitting at the red light, he couldn't help but think about Dior. She might feel that she was out there in L.A alone with no one watching her, but unbeknownst to her, she belonged to him; there was nothing that she did without his knowledge. She knew that he was a businessman with his hands in a few baskets--she just didn't know how many baskets there were. Once he made it to his house, he parked his car, locked it, and went inside. It was lonely without Dior; he missed the simple things like her smile and stepping inside the house with the smell of cooked food waiting on him. Somewhere along the way, he lost sight of making her happy.

She would wrap her arms around him when she just wanted a hug or crawl under him when he was sitting on the sofa watching ESPN. That complete silence that they shared not needing to always talk to each other, being in one's company was good enough for them. Now, he sat in the house alone regretting the fact that he was so controlling and possessive. It didn't work twenty-five years ago when his controlling rage did nothing but get the one he loved killed.

In the bathroom, he took a swift shower and did his usual routine when he was going out for the night, not being in any mood to be around so many people, but it wasn't like he had a choice--people were expecting him to show after all he was the host. As he was getting dressed, he called his driver telling him to be out front before he stepped outside. If he didn't hate anything more, it was waiting. He checked himself out in the full-length body mirror, and he was pleased with how good he looked in his blue patterned Trofeo suit. Once he was finished getting dressed, he glanced at his watch making sure he wasn't running late. He grabbed his keys and headed out the door. Outside, he saw his driver standing beside his car waiting for him to appear.

"Hello, Tony, how was your day?"

"It was fine, sir," Tony responded walking over to the passenger side door so Clyde could slide into the back seat of his new 2014 Porsche Panamera. The car was a bold black with hostage matte black rims. The interior was a lovely black that blended well with brick red seats. Getting comfortable in the leather seats, Tony shut the door and made his way around the car.

Clyde rested his head on his hands and massaged his temple trying not to let the pressure of his two businesses get the best of him. Not only did he own the real estate agency, he also owned one of the most expensive brothels and massage parlors in Los Angeles, Texas, and Las Vegas. Just recently, some of the girls had been coming up missing to only be found months later with their throats slit, so Clyde thought it was best to move the girls and add more men to security detail.

Leaning his head back on the comfortable, plush head-rest, his phone began to vibrate in his suit jacket. Taking out the phone, Clyde checked to see who it was. Reading the text message, it only stressed him out more. He was in no mood to talk to the person that was behind the text.

Before he headed towards the mansion where the harvest was taking place, he ordered Tony to stop by the nearest flower shop. Although Dior wasn't speaking to him and wanted nothing to do with him, he still wanted her to know that he was around, he was missing her, and was thinking about her. She loved yellow and white roses, so after picking thirty-six stemmed yellow and white roses and placing them in a beautiful red vase, he instructed Tony to swing by Dior's apartment before dropping him off at the mansion.

Thirty minutes later, they were at Dior's apartment complex. As they drove around looking for her car, Clyde examined the place. From the looks of it, she was in the worst area of Los Angeles. The dumpsters were overfilled with trash to where it began to run over. The smell was vile. Children were running around in nothing but dirty diapers playing in muddy water. Dope dealer was sitting on the hood of their cars passing out dope to dope fiends.

"Nobody should live in these types of conditions," Clyde mumbled to himself.

After driving around the complex for ten minutes, he ordered Tony to park. Tony did as he was told and parked a few apartments down. Clyde got out and walked towards Dior's apartment going up the stairs. He got out a pair of keys, unlocked the door, and casually walked in. What she failed to realize was the amount of power and control he had. Three days before she moved into her apartment, Clyde ordered the apartment manager to get him a key made for her apartment. He also went as far as installing cameras around her apartment. He stepped inside of her apartment, cutting on the nearest light revealing her small five hundred and ninety square foot apartment. It was smaller than what he was used to; it wasn't somewhere he would want his woman to live. He wouldn't even want his worst enemy to live in those types of conditions.

Exploring the place, he noticed old stains on the carpet; he was sure it was blood. The walls were dirty, and the paint was chipping. If he could have it his way, he would pack up all of her belongings and force her to move back to their home where he knew it was safe and livable, but if he tried to push her back, he most definitely would never see her again, so instead, he placed the vase on top of the kitchen counter with an envelope of ten thousand dollars inside with a note that read, *Should hold you for a couple of months.*

Going into her bedroom, he laid in her unmade bed

grabbing her pillow and buried his face into it. Closing his eyes, he took in her scent--a sense of calm pulsated through his body. He laid there for three minutes before getting up and went into her bathroom. He dug through her dirty laundry until he found what he was searching for--immediately taking a sniff and stuffing it into his suit pocket. Looking himself over in her body mirror, he fixed his suit and walked out of her bedroom. He left out of her apartment, locked the door behind him, and walked down the stairs. Tony opened the door for him; he slid back in.

An hour had passed, and he made it to the mansion. Getting out of the car, he walked in, greeting the men that were mingling. He sat in one of the chairs watching the men flirt with the ladies, talk, and drink. Sipping on his champagne, he looked around and noticed how beautiful the women were. They had on nothing but a gold masquerade mask and pearls that hung between their succulent breasts. Any other time, he would be joining the men in the festivities, but tonight, his mind was consumed with Dior.

Digging in his suit pocket, he took out the pair of thongs that he had gotten out of her dirty hamper and sniffed it. Closing his eyes, he imagined Dior on top of his face grinding her ass while he indulged in her delicates. His mind drifted off to one of many sexual encounters that they shared.

*Walking into the house after a long night at a banquet, Dior immediately stepped out of her heels. As soon as she stepped inside of the house kicking them to the side, she began walking up the stairs until Clyde swooped her up off her feet and carried her up the steps. Placing her on her feet, she now stood in the middle of the bedroom.*

*"I'm going to fuck you senseless tonight," he stated, running his finger slowly across her chin up to her plump lips. Taking his*

finger, she slid it into her mouth, nibbling on his finger just enough to where it hurt.

"What are you waiting for?" Dior seductively asked, looking up at him. He stood in front of her with his shirt unbuttoned, showing his perfectly sculpted chest. He grabbed her by the arm, swung her around with her back up against him, and slowly began undoing her evening gown, allowing it to fall at her feet. He stepped back up against their oak wood dresser, and in his husky, dominating tone, he told Dior to bend over. Doing as she was told, she spread her legs as far as she could and bent down from the waist. While doing so, all she could think about was her beautiful gown that was now scrunched up on the floor.

"You're so beautiful, Bubbles." He softly spoke while unzipping his pants. He began to slowly walk towards her until his dick was snuggled comfortably between her pussy, resting at her opening without entering. He took his finger and slid it down her moist slit--sliding his index finger inside. Her pussy began to drip uncontrollably as she bit down on her bottom lip trying not to scream out in pleasure.

"Do you want it?" he asked in his dominating tone.

"Yes, I want it."

"Then beg for it."

"Please...Clyde. Mmm, I want you inside of me so bad." She purred, shaking her ass.

"Mmm," he groaned, taking his finger out, placing the tip of his dick at her moist entrance. Slowly sinking his hard dick inside of her, strong pleasurable waves soared through her body,

"You feel so fucking good," Dior whispered.

He picked her up and threw her on the bed, positioning himself between her legs, forcing her to spread them farther apart. The only thing she saw was his piercing blue eyes in the moonlight beaming down on her. His hard, masculine chest moved up and down as blood rushed through his body rapidly.

*He thrust hard making her cry out in pleasure. Her creamy wetness covered his shaft. The only thing that was heard was their moans and their bodies slapping against each other. Suddenly, they both erupted, moaning together like howling wolves.*

# CLYDE

~

"Here'e, Here'e, men of the harvest, can I please have your attention? As a special gift from our very own Mr. Night, he has brought us something exquisite to end the evening. Only one lucky fool will indulge in this exquisite treat, so please help me in welcoming this beautiful jewel."

One of the men stood around the men with his arm extended out motioning for one of the security guards to bring out the young girl. She slowly walked into the massive, gold, double doors frightened. The men began whispering amongst themselves; they couldn't believe how beautiful she was. Naturally, she had curly, red hair, full lips, a curvy body, and small C-cup breasts. She wore a pink strapless mini dress with six-inch heels. All eyes were on her as she shivered from a cold breeze. As she stood there afraid, the men surrounded her like a pack of wolves. Clyde was far from interested; he just continued to sit there in his chair twirling Dior's lace panties between his fingers. The weekend he was supposed to spend with Dior, he was in

Moscow retrieving women that he won from a trafficking auction. When he looked at this woman, he knew she was going to make him a lot of money-- not only did she have beautiful, silk, pure white skin, he wanted her for himself, but knew he couldn't have her.

"Two thousand, do I have two thousand?" The man began calling out bids like an auctioneer. He shouted into the crowd of men, while they puffed on their fat cigars and drinking their whiskey.

"Three thousand!" one of the men shouted out.

"Five thousand!" another shouted, raising his fat hands up in the air with his fingers twirled around his cigar.

A tear slowly streamed down her cheeks as the men continued to bid on her like she was cattle. "One-hundred thousand!" said another.

"Woo, one-hundred thousand, do we have two-hundred, going once, going twice. Sold to the gentleman in the black hat," the auctioneer said with a loud, hardy chuckle, and the men joined him in the laugh.

Snapping his fingers, a security guard went into the room and grabbed the woman by the arm and led her out through the tall double doors into the hall taking her to another room. Opening a door, he pushed her with so much force to where she almost sprained her ankle. Shoving her into the room, he closed it and locked the door. She continued to stand there in the middle of the room confused about what just took place. She couldn't help but think about the night before. As she stood in the dark, she could hear other girls screaming. Her heart pounded harder and faster. She didn't know what was going to take place when she was taken, but now that she was here, she understood somewhat about what was about to happen to her. She was being sold off into slavery, no matter how she felt.

"Mr. Night, would you like another drink?" one of the girls asked, knocking him out of his deep thoughts. She looked down and noticed his erection, and a devilish grin crept upon her face. Without saying a word, he got up and left the party.

Leaving the party, he walked towards Tony who was sitting in the car on the phone. Clyde motioned for Tony to get off the phone and start up the car.

"Where to boss?" Tony asked, looking in the rearview mirror waiting for his orders.

"I need to go to Dior's."

Tony shook his head in approval, started up the car, and headed in the direction of Dior's apartment. Once Tony parked the car, Clyde got out and walked up to Dior's apartment, taking two stairs at a time, knocking on her door. He knew that she was in there because he could see the backlights on. He knocked for the third time, and she swung the door open.

"What do you..." Before she could get the rest of her words out, he grabbed her up, walked into the apartment, and closed the door.

"What are you doing?" Dior questioned, giving him a perplexed look.

"I told you about questioning me," he said, pulling her into him, placing his full lips on top of hers. A soft moan escaped her mouth. Wrapping his arms around her waist, he lifted her up and carried her into the bedroom.

# 5

# DIOR

*B*eing jerked out of her deep sleep by the sound of her phone going off, she reached over to her nightstand and grabbed it. She glanced at her messages to see who could be texting her so early in the morning, and that was when she realized it was her phone, internet, and light company sending her confirmation numbers from payments that were made. She knew she wasn't going crazy, but she felt like it because she hadn't paid any bills as of yet. Then, Clyde's face popped into her head. Feeling frustrated, she dialed his number.

*"Good morning,"* he said in a calm but cheerful tone.

*"What are you doing, Clyde? It's one thing to break into my house and leave money behind, but then you pay my bills. When have I asked you to do any of this for me?"*

*"I don't think someone that breaks into one's apartment would leave behind ten thousand dollars,"* he responded, disregarding her other statement.

*"Look, what we did last night was a mistake; it shouldn't have happened. I know that you feel like you gotta continue to*

*take care of me, but you don't. I'm a big girl; I can take care of myself, so please stop with everything."*

*"Is that what you're telling yourself, because the way your pussy dripped when I entered you tells me differently, and you're my woman--no matter where you go, you will always be mine. Taking care of you is what I do,"* he said with a grin.

Dior began to feel the heat coming from between her legs as he spoke about the night before. Her mind strayed off to the encounter, and she started to feel uncomfortable with the thoughts that invaded her mind. Quickly hanging up the phone, she got out of bed and went into the bathroom to take a hot shower. After finishing up with her routine, she got dressed, putting on just a white shirt and a pair of tights. Not having any plans of going anywhere, she didn't bother combing her hair.

She made her way into the kitchen and began roaming the fridge searching for something to eat, and that's when she noticed that all she had was a loaf of bread and orange juice.

"Fuck!" She huffed out loud, not feeling up to go anywhere. Grabbing her phone, she decided to make an order through Postmates. Flipping through the pages, she didn't know what she was in the mood to eat.

*Knock! Knock!*

An unexpected knock on the door alarmed her. Placing the phone down on the kitchen counter, Dior made her way to the door. "Who is it?" she asked, tiptoeing to peep through the peephole.

"It's Tony, ma'am." Tony was Clyde's driver.

"What the hell could he want?" she mumbled, opening the door to Tony standing there surrounded by bags of groceries.

"Mr. Night wanted me to deliver these bags of groceries to you."

"Um, okay, thank you..." she replied, standing there at the door looking at all the food.

"I guess come in."

She moved to the side allowing him to come in. He grabbed the bags and walked in. Taking some bags out of his cluttered hands, they both went into the kitchen.

"Thank you, Tony, I think I got it from here."

"You sure, ma'am? I would be glad to help you put everything away."

"No, that's okay, I can do it. Thank you again."

Walking Tony to the door, she locked it behind him, then headed back into the kitchen to put the rest of her groceries away.

Later that night, after her groceries were put away and the kitchen was spotless, she decided on a nice bubble bath with some excellent Jazz music. Before she could make it to her bathroom, her phone rang, so she picked it up.

*"Hello?"* she said into the phone.

*"Hey girl, what you doin'?"*

*"Nothing, I was about to jump in the tub and soak."*

*"How you been? You sound a little flustered."*

*"Girl, I don't know what I'm going to do with this Clyde. Let me tell you what happened last night. I was about to go to bed when there was a knock on my door, sounding like the police and shit. I mean, the area I'm in ain't the best, so you already know I was nervous as hell with all that loud banging and shit. I opened the door, and there he was, Mr. Night, looking good and shit. He just came to my spot like he owned shit. He treated my body like it belonged to him, and in some strange way, I believe he believes it. A part of me says it was a mistake to sleep with him, but that was the most pleasurable mistake. Every*

*time he comes around, it's like my body knows it's him, and I instantly get wet. "*

*"So, what you gon' do then, you gon' go back to him?"*

*"Hell naw, I don't want him to know that he has that kind of effect on me."*

*"I'm sure he already knows, girl. Why you think he just popped up at your spot all macho and shit? Because he knows he got it like that. Shit, I wish a nigga would come to my spot and bust down my door just to take my shit."*

*"British, this nigga is so fucking controlling, girl. I want to go back to him so bad, but his controlling ways, I can't handle."*

*"He might be a little crazy and controlling, but what man isn't, especially a man with his caliber? Shit, I know a lot of women that wouldn't mind having a man such as him to control them and spoil them at the same time. Sometimes you gotta take the good with the bad."*

*"Don't get me wrong, I understand that I can't just throw away four years. Some of those years were actually wonderful, I'm just tired of feeling like I come second to him, and always feeling like I can't do anything without his permission."*

*"Right, I understand that, but anyway, girl, enough about all that shit. I'm going out tonight to this new hookah bar called The Lounge with a couple of my girls, you wanna tag along?"*

*"Um, yeah, I've never been to a hookah lounge."*

*"I'ma pick you up around ten-ish, so be ready."*

After they both hung up the phone, Dior continued her day, until it was time for her to dressed.

b

Dior put her last touches on her outfit. Applying a little

makeup, she checked the time, and it was almost ten, which meant British would be swinging by her spot any minute. She poured herself a glass of wine as she waited. She was excited to be going out and not having to answer to anyone or explain as to why she was wearing a particular outfit out. While sitting in her recliner taking a couple sips of her Sweet Bitch Moscato Rose, there was a light tap at her door. Getting up from her chair, she sashayed over and answered the door.

"Damn girl, you lookin' dumb cute tonight," hype Dior said as they hugged each other

"Bitch, you lookin' mighty fine yourself, you ready to go?"

"Hell yea, I'm ready, let's get outta here." Dior grabbed her things and locked the door behind her.

After a forty-minute drive, they ended up on Sunset Boulevard. Sitting at the red light, she looked around at all the people that were walking up and down the strip. Once they parked, they both took out their compact mirrors to apply an extra layer of lip gloss. They got out the car and made their way up to the door. The line wasn't as long as they would have thought with it being the grand opening and shit. As they walked inside the bar, British and Dior immediately fell in love; the atmosphere was friendly-- it was small, but cozy, and there was a band already set up for the night. British and Dior decided on sitting at the bar to wait for the other girls. Ordering their drinks, British got a text message from one of her friends.

"Guess it's just you and me tonight, girl," British said as she replied to the text.

"Wha...what happened?"

"Sasha said her man wanted to spend some time

together tonight since he's on vacation, and Dior said her man was taking her out to eat."

"Damn, everybody spendin' time with their man tonight, huh?"

"Yep, guess it's just us single girls," British said as she clanked her henny up against Dior's glass of Gimlet.

"I gotta go to the restroom, watch my drink and make sure nobody slips nothin' in it." Dior couldn't help but shake her head at British and her dramatic ways. She took out her phone and snapped a couple of pictures of her drink and the bar she was sitting at along with some selfies to post on Instagram.

"Would you mind if I sit here?" a deep voice asked, startling Dior. She looked up and was memorized by how handsome he was. What he had was a deep chocolate complexion, tall, about six-foot-two, with a skinny, muscular build, and nicely dressed--she couldn't get over how handsome he was.

"Um, sure, help yourself," she finally replied.

"What is that you're drinking?" he asked, trying to start small talk.

"Um, Gimlet," she responded with a smile. He smiled back almost knocking her over with his deep ass dimples.

"I'm Jayvon."

"Nice to meet you, Jayvon. I'm Dior."

"Dior, what a beautiful name."

Time seemed to fly by as they both sat and talked. She looked at her phone and realized that British wasn't back. Roaming the room with her eyes, she spotted British on the dance floor with a couple of white men. The way they were dressed, they could have been essential businessmen, the suite they wore were nothing that could be bought from Dillard's. If Dior didn't learn anything from the four-year relationship with Clyde, she knew an expensive suit when she saw one.

"Would you like to dance? I see you eyeing the dance floor."

"No, I was looking for my friend; she was supposed to come back over this way, but I see she made a little detour."

He looked over to the same direction as Dior, then looked back over at her, grabbed her by the hand and led her to the dance floor.

"I'm not that good of a dancer," Dior said as Jayvon was ignoring her, he then turned her around to face him, pulled her in by the waist, and began to two-stepping.

"For someone that isn't a good dancer, you seem to be doing pretty good," he said as he ran his hand up the middle of her back. Dior rested her head on his chest closing her eyes, listening to his heart beating. Even though she was having the time of her life with this stranger, she couldn't stop thinking about Clyde and how much she was missing him. Things like this were the stuff she had always wanted to do with him, but he was always too busy or never home. After the band finished their song, Jayvon escorted her back to the bar.

"Excuse me, I have to go to the restroom," Jayvon said as he excused himself. As he walked away, she couldn't help but to check out his ass. As she waited for him to return, she decided to send Clyde a text message.

**11:40 p.m Dior: I was just thinking about you and realized how much I miss you.**

"Is everything okay?" Jayvon asked with a smile, showing off his dimples.

"Yes, everything is fine," she answered, stuffing her phone back into her purse.

"Who is this tall glass of chocolate milk?" British asked, interrupting their conversation

"This is Jayvon, Jayvon, this is my best friend, British."

"Well, hello there, sexy," British said as she brushed herself up against him, making Dior feel a little uncomfortable. Whenever British had one too many drinks, she became the community pussy.

"Nice to meet you." He shook her hand then put his attention back on Dior. She was shocked at the way he just curved British like that. She looked at him with a weird expression. British ordered herself two more shots, knocked them back, and went back on the dance floor, popping her ass like they were at some club.

"What's wrong?" he questioned.

"Nothing, I've just never seen a man curve her the way you just did. Most men..."

"Hold up, shorty, I'm not most men, so you don't even gotta finish that statement, so back to us, are you from here?" he asked, ordering himself another drink.

"No, I'm actually from Texas, I moved to Pacific Palisades about six months ago."

"Texas, huh? That's what's up. I'm from Texas myself."

"Really! What part?"

"Dallas."

"No shit! I'm from Dallas also."

"That's what's up, you see it was meant for the both of us to link up tonight. It's still early, how about we get up outta here and get something to eat? There's this spot that stays open twenty-four-seven."

Dior took out her phone and sent British a text. British wasn't paying any type of attention to Dior; she knew it would be a while before she was being missed.

**Dior: He's asking me to go have some drinks with him**

**tonight.** Dior looked up from her phone to sees Jayvon texting away on his phone as well.

"I hope it's nothing important."

"Nah, just taking care of some business back home, you know how family can be. You ready?" he asked, taking her by the hand and escorting her out the bar.

"What made you want to come to L.A?"

"I'm here on business. I don't know how long, but I hope as long as I am here, you can keep me company and show me some of your favorite spots."

"I think I would like that," she said. As she got into his car, she was surprised by the type of car he was driving; she loved the brand-new smell that it still had. For the remainder of that night, they spent their time at the diner eating, laughing, and getting to know each other.

# 6

# DIOR

*A*s she stirred around in bed, Dior quickly opened her eyes as the smell of bacon and eggs evaded her nostrils. With a smile on her face, she slid out of bed grabbing her robe and headed towards the kitchen.

*Damn, he looks good standing over the stove,* she thought to herself as she stood there in the kitchen doorway watching him in nothing but blue and white basketball shorts. He had a nice little body, nothing as spectacular as Clyde's, but it was nice. He had a nice, light-skinned complexion; she wondered what he was mixed with. It reminded her of the actor Jesse Williams just without the pretty eyes. She could tell that he had just gotten his hair cut; his fade was clean-- he didn't have much facial hair, just a little on his chin. She stood there in a trance looking him up and down daydreaming about the previous night. Ever since they met at the bar two months ago, it seemed they couldn't keep their hands off each other. Jayvon would find himself spending more and more time at Dior's spot than his own.

"Good morning," she finally said, taking a step closer

towards him and wrapping her arms around his waist running her hands up to his chest.

"Good morning, beautiful. I hope I didn't wake you.

"The smell of bacon is what woke me," she said grabbing a piece off the plate as she started setting the table for breakfast.

"What else did you cook for breakfast?"

"Not much, just some cheddar grits, bacon, eggs, and waffles."

"Okay, we got a chef up in here," Dior said with a laugh.

"Nah, nothing like that; I love to cook, and thought I would cook you something good this morning. Also, I hope you don't mind, but I did a little grocery shopping early this morning, most of the food in the fridge has almost gone bad, so I got rid of the bad and restocked."

"Oh, yeah, well you know I'm not much of a cook. I've been so busy with work and trying to get into a school that I haven't had time to do any grocery shopping."

After they both finished breakfast, Dior gathered the dirty dishes and began to clean them while Jayvon sat in the living room flipping through channels. She was starting to feel some sense of normality. It'd been four months since she last heard from Clyde--a part of her missed him and wondered where he could be, but then, another part of her hoped he never came back and stayed gone for good.

While doing the dishes, Jayvon's phone went off. She looked over at him, and just by his facial expression, she knew something was wrong.

"Is everything okay?" she asked drying her hands on a dishtowel and walked towards him.

"Um, yeah, it' just work. I was planning on spending my day with you, but something has happened at the construction site; I gotta go. What are you doing later tonight?"

"Well, nothing, I guess I'ma hang here at the house, do some laundry, and get some cleaning done, why?"

"I shouldn't be at the site for too long, so I was wondering if I could come back over when everything is done, and I'll cook dinner for you," he said with a soft smile.

"Oh, so you know how to cook dinner too? Dang, and why are you single again?"

"If things keep going as they are, I hope to not be single for long," he responded with a devilish grin. Dior couldn't help but smile at his remark. She was willing to give it a try; she was craving a relationship where she felt like she was more than property.

"Aight, I'ma call you in about two hours to check up on you," he said kissing her, before going into the bedroom to jump in the shower. She smiled at the thought of her being with someone like Jayvon; he was charming, strong, open-minded, great sense of humor, and easy to talk to. In only two weeks, she found herself falling in love with him.

In a deep sleep, Dior suddenly woke up. Rolling over, she grabbed her phone off the nightstand to check the time. To her surprise, it was only one in the morning. Getting out of bed, she grabbed her robe and headed towards the kitchen. Opening the fridge, Dior stood there trying to decide what she was going to snack on. Taking out the pint of mint ice cream, grabbing a spoon, she stood in front of the fridge and took a couple of big scoops.

"What are you doing up?"

Startled, she turned around to face Jayvon standing there with his eyes barely open; she couldn't help but to smile. "I don't know, I just woke up and had a taste for something sweet."

"Well, can I have some?" he asked, walking towards her. Dior took the spoon out of the carton and raised it up to his mouth. He parted his lips, but she detoured the spoon to his chest. She began to smear the ice cream across his hairless chest.

"Oops, let me get that," she muttered licking it off him slowly as she looked up at him seductively. She pushed him up against the fridge twirling her tongue around his nipples and down the middle of his chest, kissing around his belly button, then continued down to his dick. The remainder of that night they spent ravishing each other's bodies until the sun came up.

Calling into work that morning, she was worn out from Jayvon tapping that ass that early; she wasn't in the mood to deal with people that morning. Dior wanted to spend that day preparing a romantic dinner for Jayvon. After Jayvon left for work, she scooted out of bed and got dressed to begin her day. Needing help on ideas of what to cook that night, she spent a few hours surfing the internet looking for recipes; she wanted something other than a simple steak and potatoes. Deciding on lemon chicken and piccata pasta, she scribbled down the recipe, grabbed her keys and purse, and headed to the grocery store. After she gathered everything that she needed for the night along with some red roses and white candles and white wine to go with the dinner, she headed home feeling excited about that night.

～

As they sat at the table enjoying their dinner, Jayvon's phone rang, and Dior was starting to get annoyed. Since he'd been home, his phone hadn't stopped dinging.

"Who is that that keeps texting you?" she questioned.

"Nobody, its just work," he replied, but Dior knew better but decided to ignore it. She spent all day cooking a good meal and didn't want to let his phone ruin her evening.

"Whoever it is, could you please tell them that you're eating dinner with your woman, and they can wait until the morning."

"I can't control what people do, bae," Jayvon replied as he continued to text away on his phone. By that time, Dior wasn't in the mood anymore. Picking up her plate from the table, she got up and placed it in the sink. Leaving out of the kitchen, she looked over to Jayvon who was still sitting at the dining room table consumed by his texting. For the remainder of that night, Dior cleaned the kitchen, took a shower, and went to bed. She wasn't upset that her plan for a romantic date night didn't go as planned, she was more hurt that Jayvon couldn't give her his undivided attention that night.

"Ugh, where is he?" Dior huffed as she paced back and forth waiting for Jayvon to pick her up from work. It'd been a long nine-hour shift, and all she could think about was soaking her body in some hot water. Getting her phone out of her purse, she redialed his number only to get voicemail.

"Would you like a ride?" Dior's manager asked, stepping towards her with paper in his hand.

"No, my boyfriend is picking me up."

"You've been out here for an hour now, Dior. Are you sure you don't want me to drop you off at home?"

"Yes, I'm sure, thank you."

"Well, it's getting dark--I don't want you out here much longer. I will leave you the keys to the office, and you can wait inside." As he was handing her the keys to the office a car squeaking as it was turning into the parking lot came into eyeshot, and when she looked closer, she realized that it was Jayvon.

"Here he is right here," she said to her manager as she grabbed her purse and walked towards the curb waiting for him to pull up.

"I'm so sorry, baby; shit was crazy at the construction site, then I had an unexpected meeting I had to attend. I didn't expect for it to last over an hour." Jayvon quickly explained, praying she wouldn't get upset. After she got in the car, the anger she felt for him disappeared. She was happy to see him, and she couldn't be upset with him for too long.

"What you wanna do tonight?" he asked, driving out of the parking lot.

"I just want to go home and take a hot bubble bath and relax, maybe have a couple of drinks."

"Do you wanna go out or stay in tonight?" he asked, stopping at the stop sign.

"We can go out somewhere. It's Friday, and I don't want to spend the rest of my Friday inside."

"Aight, I've found this new spot I think you're gonna love," he stated, taking her hand in his.

Once they made it home, Dior went straight to the bedroom where three dozen yellow roses were waiting for her along with a gift basket from Bath and Body Works.

"Oh my gosh, is all this for me?" she questioned with excitement in her voice, picking up the roses, and putting them up to her nose. "I love yellow roses--how did you know?"

"I don't know, you didn't seem like a red and pink roses type of girl."

"I...I don't know what to say. What is all this for though?"

"Does there need to be a reason, beautiful? You're my girl; there's gonna be a lot of days like this where you come home from work all tired and shit, to only have something special waiting on you."

"I...I just don't know what to say, Jayvon, thank you." Putting down the vase, she went over to him wrapping her arms around him giving him a deep kiss, and he welcomed it. Placing his hands under her ass, he lifted her up and walked over to the bed as he unbuttoned her red blouse. He flipped her over and unzipped her black pencil skirt. He pulled them down as she wiggled her ass trying to get them to come off. She was now in nothing but her thong and bra set she ordered from Fredrick's of Hollywood. Softly, he kissed her on the back of her neck, running his tongue down the middle of her back until he was at her ass.

"You're so beautiful," he moaned while grabbing ahold of her ass and slapping it. She yelped in excitement. He smirked at her moans; he was about to give her something that he knew her body was craving. Jayvon tugged on her thong with his teeth pulling them to the side and buried his face between her ass cheeks. Sticking his tongue out, he started licking around her booty hole.

"Ohh, baby, I ain't showered yet," Dior stated as she tried to get up, but Jayvon wasn't having that.

"I love smelling and tasting you natural, so be still and let me satisfy my hunger."

He proceeded to eat her out from the back making her toes curl as she could feel her passion begin to rise. He slid her panties off putting her on her knees where he had more access to her pretty pearls. Sticking his tongue out, he began to slide the tip from pussy to ass and back to her pussy

"Shit, baby, that feels so fucking good." She purred.

He rose up and flipped her over onto her back; Jayvon positioned himself between her legs, and she could feel his bulge underneath his jeans, which she wondered why he still had them on.

"Take them off," she commanded pulling on them. He did as he is told and began to undress. She licked her lips as she gazed at his fully erect nine inches.

"Wait," she said, stopping him from climbing back onto the bed. "I wanna watch you jack off." She spoke in a soft tone.

Without hesitation, he grabbed ahold of his meat and began stroking it. Watching him please himself turned her on, she began to play with her drenched pussy sliding her finger inside, then she took it out, and he leaned down and sucked her juices off her finger. Dior flipped him to where she was now mounting him; he leaned back on the head-board—they were now facing each other. Kissing one another passionately, their tongues danced as he cupped her breast. Reaching around, he unbuttoned her bra allowing her breasts to fall as he sucked on her nipples. She grabbed ahold of his dick and slowly inched her way down onto it. Dior took in a deep gasp as he filled her up,

"Mmm! Baby, your dick feels so good," Dior softly moaned. She stared into his eyes as she slowly bounced up and down on his meat. Squeezing her muscles around his dick, she held onto it as if her life depended on it.

"Damn baby, you 'bout to make me nut." He grunted, wrapping his arm around her waist. He flipped her over onto her stomach, and she knew what was about to come.

She arched her back like a good girl as he shoved his massive dick inside of her. Jayvon grabbed a handful of her ass and started to pound away; all that could be heard was their flesh slapping up against each other.

He got a hand full of Dior's hair as his thrusts got stronger and shorter, giving her pussy no mercy. Dior took ahold of the bed sheets as she began to feel herself about to explode.

"Fuck! Baby! I'm about to cum!" she screamed out as her legs began to convulse.

"Yes! Cum for me, baby." He grunted, slapping her on the ass, digging deeper into her wetness, juices escaping her pussy and sliding down his balls, and suddenly, they both exploded at the same time. His fast, rapid thrusts weren't slow and gentle, they were feverishly hard and exhilarating. She collapsed on the bed, and he landed on top of her with his dick still inside of her.

After their sexcapades, Dior got up and went into the bathroom picking the gift set off the floor. Turning the water on in the tub, she threw one of the bath bombs in the water allowing the water to fill up a little more and slid in. The hot water surrounded her body, causing her to sink into the tub and exhale deeply.

"Would you like some company?" a naked Jayvon asked, holding a wine glass filled with her favorite wine and a Corona. Dior lifted up her body, motioning for him to slide in behind her. "So, I take it we're not going out tonight," Dior said with a giggle.

# 7

# DIOR

"*L*ook, babe, I'm not happy about it either, but I have to get back to Texas. My boss just called and is expecting me to be in the office tomorrow morning. I've already purchased my plane ticket for seven tonight, so I need to start packing my things, but I promise I will be back next week," Jayvon said as he held an upset Dior in his arms.

"I understand, don't mean I have to like it. How about I come with you?"

"Naw, you'll be lonelier there than here; it's crazy in Texas. I'm never home, always working, and shit, and when I'm not working, I'm sleeping. These pasts five months that I've spent here with you have been nothing but amazing. When I come back, maybe we can sit down and talk about us moving into a bigger spot. I know that we've only been together for five months now, but I feel like we've grown so much as a couple, I want us to start building a foundation for our future."

The things that Jayvon was saying to Dior were sounding so good, and she couldn't believe that she found a good man that was ready to settle down and start building.

"That sounds like something I would be willing to discuss when you come back."

"Good, now, are you gonna help me pack?" Dior agreed and went towards the bedroom. Going into the closet, she grabbed his clothes and started to fold them, placing them neatly into the suitcase he brought with him five months ago. It was now time for him to be at the airport. "You want me to drop you off? It'll give us more time together," she said, trying to fight back her tears.

"You already know how this L.A traffic be." He grabbed his things, she grabbed her purse, and they both headed out the door locking it behind them.

She made it back home after dropping Jayvon off at the airport. She was feeling more alone than she had in a long time. Before leaving, Jayvon did some grocery shopping to hold her up until he got back; he already knew that she wasn't going to do it. Going into the kitchen, she opened the fridge; there was nothing that was appealing. Taking a deep sigh, she closed it and decided on just a glass of water. She went into her bedroom with the glass of water in her hand. Sitting it on the table beside her bed, she crawled into bed curling up next to the pillow that Jayvon slept on. Dior found herself dozing off until her cell phone began to ring jarring her out of her sleep. She reached over to the other side of the bed and answered it without even checking the Caller ID.

*"Hello,"* she said in a saddened tone.

*"What's wrong with you, girl? You sound all down and shit."*

"Jayvon left," she said to British on the other line.

"What! He left you? I told you these niggas out here in these streets ain't no good."

"No, I mean he left to go back to Dallas."

"What he do that for?"

"Something about his boss needing him back down there. Girl, I don't know. I wish I could have gone back with him though."

"Why didn't you?"

"He said that I would hardly see him since he would always be at the office, shit like that, but shit, Brit, I don't give a fuck about all that. He wouldn't be at the job twenty-four-seven though; there has to be a time where he would have to come home though, right? Plus, I haven't been home for a few years now; I could spend that time with my mother, she would be so surprised to see me."

"Girl, if you don't get your shit and go see yo' mama and yo' man and get off this phone."

"Yea, I should, huh?"

"Hell yea, you should. Hhit me up if you need a ride to the airport."

"Alright, I'ma book my ticket right now and let you know what's up."

British and Dior finished their conversation before hanging up. Later that night, Dior booked her plane ticket online and began packing her clothes to leave in the morning. She called her mother to tell her the good news, but there was no answer, so she decided to surprise her instead.

Dior got off the plane and made her way to the exit, with her luggage trailing behind her. She goy out her cell phone and called up Jayvon to let him know that she was in Dallas, and she needed to be picked up, hoping that he would more happy to see her as she was to see him.

"*Hello,* he answered.

"*Hey baby, I need you to come pick me up.*"

"*Where you at?*" he asked, sounding a bit confused.

"*I'm here in Dallas. I got lonely in L.A and decided to come home.*"

The phone suddenly went silent. She took the phone from her ear to check to see if the call was lost.

"*Hello?*" she said into the phone.

"*What about your job?*" Jayvon finally answered, but it wasn't the answer that she was expecting. She just told him that she was in Dallas, and all he was worried about was her job.

"*I had some vacation time saved up, so I decided to take a vacation and come here to visit my mama and hope to see you while I'm here.*" Jayvon paused for a few before responding.

"*Ight, I'm on my way,*" he said before hanging up.


An hour had passed, and Jayvon still hadn't shown up. She got out her phone and called him again, but this time, he didn't pick up. Taking a deep breath, she decided to get one of the taxis that was sitting outside. Sliding into a taxi, she told him where she wanted to go. He nodded his head in approval, started up the car, and headed towards the destination.

Once she arrived at her mother's home, she looked out the window taking in the beautiful house she grew up in. She was surprised to see the lawn was still beautifully mani-cured; the yellow rose bushes had bloomed, and the oranges from the orange tree that stood on the side of the house were starting to fall. A smile crept up on her face as she was so happy to finally be home. Childhood memories began to flood her memory bank.

Dior paid the taxi driver, got out, and waited for him to pop the trunk. After he popped the trunk, he got out and helped her with the luggage. Dior carried her baggage up to the front steps, rang the doorbell, and waited for an answer; she knew her mother was at home because her car was parked in the driveway. She rang the doorbell for the third time, ultimately getting the attention of someone to come and open the door, but the person that answered caught Dior off guard. It was a Hispanic woman in purple scrubs with her hair in a high ponytail.

"Hello, uhm...is my mother here?" Dior examined the strange woman that stood in front of her with a smile on her face.

"Oh, you must be Dior? Please, come in; I'm sorry, I was in the kitchen making your mother something to eat."

"Is she okay? Why would she need someone to cook for her? She isn't the type to ask for help."

"You haven't heard?"

"Heard what?"

"I'll let her tell you."

Dior looked at the woman strangely and began to walk up the stairs to her mother's bedroom. Softly knocking on her door, she opened it.

"Mama," she called out to Eleanor as she slowly opened the door. The sight that came upon her turned her stomach into a million knots, and tears immediately appeared in her eyes. Taking a deep breath, she wiped away the tears, attempting to control the knots that were in her stomach.

"Hey mama, it's me, Dior," she quietly said walking towards the bed that was enclosed by IV poles and breathing devices. Sitting beside her mother, she couldn't believe that this beautiful and energetic woman was now lying there, skin and bones. Afraid of placing all her weight on the bed in fear of breaking her, Dior gently took hold of her small, fragile hands and placed them inside of hers.

"Why didn't you call me and tell me that you were sick?" Dior whimpered as tears suddenly fell onto the top of Eleanor's hand.

"She didn't want to worry you; she knew if she called, you would've came running home, leaving your life in L.A behind," the nurse explained with a tray of food and a syringe in her hand.

"What's wrong with her, what happened?"

"She has stage four lung cancer; she refused chemo-therapy, so all we can do now is make her as comfortable as possible."

"When was the last time my sister been here to see her?"

"About five months ago when she hired a live-in nurse. She claimed that she's too busy to come by and take care of her."

"Too busy to see our mom? That's so typical of Dajah always finding a way out."

The remainder of the night, Dior unpacked her belongings in her childhood bedroom. Being in Dallas was only supposed to be for a couple of days, but now that Dior had found out about Eleanor's health, she decided to stay home. After she unpacked, she called British to ask her if she could be at her apartment for the moving company so her things could be moved out of her condo. While speaking to British, her phone beeped. She checks the Caller ID and realized that it was Jayvon. She ended the call with British and clicked over.

*"What do you want?"* she answered feeling irritated all over again.

*"Look, babe, I know I fucked up, and I'm sorry; I couldn't get away. I told you before leaving L.A that I'm going to be very busy here in Dallas, and that shit wasn't a lie. I've been here in this office since arriving yesterday morning, signing deals, firing and hiring, meetings after meetings. I'm so fucking tired, but check this, I want to make it up to you if you would like. I would love to take you out to dinner tonight.*

*"I don't know, Jayvon; my mom is extremely ill, and..."*

*"Say no more; I will order something and bring it there to you, how does that sound?"* Dior paused for a moment thinking it over.

*"Yea, alright, but don't think for a moment this is gonna make things alright between us; I'm still furious at you."* She sassed before giving him the address to where she was staying.

Forty minutes passed, and suddenly, a knock was at the door. Rushing up off the sofa she checked herself in the mirror first before answering the door and swinging the door open with a big smile on her face. Then suddenly, her smile turned into a frown.

"Were you expecting someone, or are you just happy to see your sister?"

"What do you want, Dajah?"

"Excuse me? Is that how you speak to your sister after years of not seeing or speaking to her?"

"I'm sorry, of course not; I wasn't expecting you so late. I was hoping for someone else," Dior explained, embracing Dajah with a hug.

"I see you wastin' no time bringing a man over to Eleanor's home, huh?" Dajah frowned while walking around the house to examine the house like she was a social worker.

"I know you ain't come over here to welcome me home, so why are you here?"

"That's the reason why I came by; the nurse called to tell me that you were home, and you told her to go home, so I decided to come by to see what your motives are. Are you planning on staying to take care of Eleanor, or are you just down here for some dick?"

"What's it to you, though Dajah, and when did you start calling our mother by her name?"

"I don't need you coming home disrupting everything. I already have everything set the way it needs to be, so if you're coming back home to take care of Eleanor, then I hope you don't expect me to drop everything that I'm doing--my career and life to help you with her. She doesn't need that much help anyway, just someone to keep her propped up and keep her ass clean."

"Now why would I ever ask Ms.."

"Mrs." Dajah corrected Dior letting her know that she had gotten married, flashing her the Vera Wang one-carat diamond ring. Dior was taken aback for a moment.

"Oh wow, you got married?"

"Yes, and he is a wonderful man--a man that only a woman like myself could attract."

"Anyway, congrats, Dajah, but you ain't gotta worry about me needing or wanting any of your help; I got it from here. It's almost time for mama's bath; are you staying to help, or what?

"Oh, God no; you wouldn't catch me wiping that woman's ass." Dior was about tired of her sister disrespecting her mother. Dior's phone rang, so she looked to see who it was and stuffed her phone back into her pocket.

"You need to go, Dajah. My man is on his way, and I don't need you here scaring him away."

"Yo' man? When you get a man?"

"None of your business, now will you please leave? I think we have said enough for tonight; I'll call you some-time this week," Dior said rushing Dajah out of the door.

Twenty minutes after Dajah left, there was another knock at the door. Opening the door, it was the person she wanted to see.

"Hey, baby!" Jayvon said greeting Dior with a kiss on the cheek; he could sense that something was bothering her.

"What's bothering you, babe?" he asked, handing her the bag of Chinese food.

"Nothing," she replied, but he knew she was lying; she didn't sound as excited as she did over the phone earlier.

"I know you still mad at me about today, and I'm sorry."

"No, it's not that, shit happens, I understand. I was upset, but I'm over it now. It's just.... my sister. She showed up before you came by and reminded me all too well why I moved away from home in the first place. She's so fucking disrespectful to not only me, but to our mother. I don't care that she hates me, but disrespecting the woman that birthed us isn't going to happen while I'm here." Dior vented to Jayvon.

For the remainder of that night, they both sat in the living room enjoying their Chinese food and watching a few movies until they fell asleep on the couch. As she was cuddled up against Jayvon, his phone vibrated, waking her up. She nudged him to try to wake him to let him know that he had a message, but he was dead to the world. She was beginning to get peeved as his phone continued to vibrate. Dior dug into his pocket and got out his phone. Looking at the screen, she saw a name that was familiar to her, so she clicked on the preview of the text to bring it up and began to read the text message.

HER: BABE, WHEN ARE YOU COMING HOME? I GOT OFF WORK
EARLY AND CAME HOME, AND YOU WEREN'T HERE.

Without replying, she scrolled up to read the past
messages. Feeling heartbroken, with so much force, she
slapped Jayvon out of his sleep hard enough where spit
swung out of his mouth.

"What the fuck you do that for?" Jayvon hissed as he
grabbed ahold of his burning cheek.

"You need to get the fuck outta my house right the fuck
now. I can't believe you, Jayvon, this entire time!" Dior
shouted as she hopped up from the sofa and began to throw
shit at him.

"Yo, calm the fuck down and tell me what the fuck is
going on. I ain't done shit but bring you something to eat. I
been right fucking here this entire time, so what the fuck is
your problem?" He sneered. Without replying to him, she
grabbed the nearest thing and chucked it at his head,
connecting it upside his head. He stumbled back from the
impact of the heavy ashtray. Blood started to trickle down
his face from the deep gash on his forehead.

"Get the fuck out before I fucking kill you, and take your
fucking phone. Oh, and tell your fucking wife, my sister, I
said hello."

"Sister, what the fuck you talkin' about? Who's your
sister?"

"Your wife, you dumb fuck, now leave!" Dior roared. She
grabbed a glass to throw at him, but when she threw it, she
missed his head by an inch as he hurried out the door. The
door shut, and Dior fell to her knees with tears falling down
her face.

"What the fuck, this whole time he's been married to my
sister. How the fuck did I not know that shit? ARGH!" she
screamed out as her heart ached.

# 8

# DIOR

*D*ior had been home for the past month. As the time passed, so did her mother's health. Eleanor was now fully dependent on the breathing machines and eating tubes. Hearing that the breathing machine was what was keeping her alive and the pain that she was enduring was the worst news that Dior had gotten from the doctor. Although her sister was all for pulling the plug and ending their mother's life, Dior wasn't.

She felt as if she was going to wake up any moment and get better, but the reality was she wasn't. That night, Dior spent in Eleanor's room sitting beside her bed, wishing she could have one moment to tell her how much she loved her, but the time never came. The next morning, Dior made the decision to pull the plug on her mother; it was a difficult decision for her, but she couldn't bare seeing her hooked up to plugs. Her soul was now gone, and the only thing that was there was her body. Early that morning, Dior called her doctor letting him know that she was ready to end her mother' slife.

"This is my husband Jozua," Dajah introduced her husband to Dior as she stepped inside the church. Words wouldn't come out of her mouth as she stood there in shock; all she could do was stare at this man that her sister called Jozua. She looked around the church hoping cameras would pop out, alerting her that she was being punked, but that didn't happen. She waited for this man to say something, but nothing came out of his mouth

She stood there in disbelief; she didn't know what to say or do. A part of her wanted to turn around and just run. Another part of her wanted to go into attack mode and claw Jayvon's eyes out. Standing there seeing her fucking sister all booed up to the man that was supposed to be hers made her sick to her stomach.

"Excuse me, I need to go to the bathroom," Dior said, walking towards the bath room. Walking in, she darted towards the stall and sat on the toilet putting her head into her hands trying to control her breathing. She shut her eyes and counted to ten. "It's going to be okay, Chanel. Get yourself together, not here at your mother's funeral, not now, Dior."

She tried to coach herself into not crying, calling herself by both of her names, trying to trigger the parts of her that were less stressed and less afraid.

Not wanting to mess up her makeup, Dior took a few moments to collect herself before walking out. After ten minutes, she was ready to get the day over with. Walking towards the sink, she turned it on and ran the water over her hands. The cold water on her hands felt good, so she left it there longer than expected. Turning the water off, she dried her hands and was about to walk out the bathroom until the door swung open, almost knocking her off her feet. "Oh, I am so sorry," an older woman said.

"It's alright," Dior replied with a soft smile.

"You're her baby girl, aren't you?" the older woman asked.

"Yes, I'm Dior."

"Well, praise God. You know before your mother went home to the good lord, she prayed every day for you, always asking for special prayer for you at church, always talking about you at our bible study. Your mother loved you more than her last breath. Between you and me, she loved you more than that wicked sister of yours. Lord forgive me, but that sister of yours is something special, and I don't mean that in a nice way."

"Yes, Dajah has her flaws, but under all that hardness, she has a kind heart. I wish I arrived home sooner, you know? Now that she is gone, I have no reason to be here. The love of my life isn't who I thought he was."

"Baby girl, let this old woman tell you something. Our good lord will bring and take people out of our lives for a purpose. We don't know that reason, but believe you me, there's a reason for everything. You pray and ask for guidance, and he will show you the way, but listen to me blabbering on, my daughter always says I talk too much."

Dior couldn't help but chuckle at the old woman. She was right though--HE took people out of your life just like he put them in.

"I will see you out there, stay strong. I better use the toilet before I piss myself. These depends only hold so much," the woman said before walking into the stall.

Dior left out of the bathroom. The deacon was waiting on her to escort her to her seat in front of her mom's casket. Sliding her arm in the deacon's arm, he slowly began to walk towards the front of the church. Dior felt her knees buckle under her. Before she fell back, she felt an extra pair of arms wrapping around her.

"I got you," he softly whispered into her ear. She looked up and was surprised by who it was. *How the hell does he always find me?* she asked her self.

"Where did you come from?" she questioned, taking her seat.

"I was out on business when I heard your mother passed; I'm very sorry, Dior that I wasn't here sooner for you."

"So, you been keepin' tabs on me?"

"We'll talk about this later. Here, drink this." She grabbed the water bottle and took a couple of big gulps. Her head was in a complete whirlwind; everything was happening all too fast. Her mother passing, finding out Jayvon was living a double life with two different names, and now Clyde showing up out of nowhere. Suddenly, she was feeling her life turning into a complete shit fest.

For the remainder of the funeral, she quietly sat with Clyde on one side of her, and Jayvon or Jozua, the name Dajah introduced him as on the other side. She sat there staring at her mother's beautiful casket; it was a gorgeous, solid cherry hardwood with a high gloss finish. It was also surrounded by standing cross flowers. On top of her coffin were some white roses, hybrid lilies, and monte casino, lavender cremones. The turn out was more than she could ever wish for. She glanced over at her sister and saw not one tear fall from her eyes.

"Fucking bitch," Dior mumbled.

"Did you say something?" Clyde questioned with a risen brow.

"No," Chanel responded by directing her attention back to the preacher.

Once everything was over, the deacons got up and gathered around the casket to carry it outside. Dior was the first one to walk behind the coffin. Clyde took hold of her by her waist and helped her out the building. Dior watched as Dajah and Jozua got into the limo.

"Can you take me there?" she asked looking up at Clyde.

"Yeah, let's go," he said walking over to the car with a waiting Tony standing in front of the car as usual.

"Hello, ma'am, my condolences."

"Thank you, Tony."

As Dior got in the car with Clyde, Jozua was standing beside the limo watching her exchange words with this man. This man looked very familiar, but he couldn't quite put his finger on it. "Come on, what are you doing?" Dajah pouted sticking her head out of the door. Jozua finally got into the limo.

"Where's my sister?" Dajah questioned, taking her compact mirror out of her purse to make sure her makeup was still in place.

"She drove with someone else."

"Oh, really? Hmm...I wonder if it was her boyfriend."

"Boyfriend?" Jozua repeated

"Yeah, that night I popped up to the house, she said she was meeting with her boyfriend. Of course, I didn't stay around to see who it was; I don't have time to be concerned with her personal life."

"Well, she was sitting beside someone."

"Oh, really?" Dajah tried to think back if she could remember seeing Dior sitting beside a man.

"Now that I think of it, I do remember her sitting beside

this good-looking white man." Jozua looked over at his wife as she talked about the stranger.

"I wonder who he could be, he looked like money. I couldn't imagine my sister catching someone with money, that's so out of her league."

After everyone made it to the burial site, they all got out of their cars and walked towards the other people that were standing around the casket. As Dior stood in front of her mother's casket, Clyde wrapped his arm around her waist, pulling closer to her, wanting her to know that he was there and he wasn't going anywhere. As the preacher prayed one last time, Dajah found her way over to where they were with Jozua behind her.

"Are you going to introduce us?" Dajah asked, extending her hand for Clyde to shake it.

"Not at my mother's funeral, no," Dior replied, not taking her eyes off the preacher.

"Today is the perfect day to introduce me to your lover boy." Dior couldn't help but to roll her eyes at her sister's remark.

"This is Clyde Night, Clyde this my sister, Dajah." Dior quickly introduced them as she walked towards her mother's casket to throw three red roses into the ground and to say her last goodbye.

"Oh, my God, Jozua, do you know who this is? He's the owner of Night estate. It is so nice to meet you, sir. I would have never thought I would be meeting my boss at my mother's funeral," Dajah excitingly said.

As Dajah continued to speak to Clyde, Jozua made his way over to where Dior was standing. "I'm sorry," he softly said as he stood beside her.

"There's nothing for you to be sorry about, Jay.. Jozua.

You're a foul muthafucka, and I would appreciate it if you would back the fuck up."

"Look, Dior, I understand you're upset with me.."

"Upset, nigga, I'm far from upset. Not only did you lie to me about being married, but you had me going around here believing your lies. That shit right there is some fuck boy shit. if you think I'ma lay around and continue to fuck you while you're laying up under my sister, you got me all the way fucked up," Dior said as she turned and walked back towards Clyde.

"Nice to meet you, and yes, I'm just here as support is all," Clyde said as his attention was towards Dior and Jozua. He had a problem with Jozua standing so close to his woman; he had the urge to go over there and throw that skinny boy in the hole with their mother.

"Hello," Dajah said trying to put Clyde's attention back on her. He darted his eyes back onto a babbling Dior, pretending that he was listening to what she was saying, although he wasn't interested.

"Ha-ha, there you are. You zoned out there for a moment, but like I was saying, I just want to thank you for being our support system. my family and I really appreciate it, and to show my gratitude, I would love for you to come to my home for dinner sometime this week."

Clyde hesitantly agreed. Dajah gave him her number and address to her place, and left as Dior was walking back towards them.

"What was she talking about?"

"Nothing, she wants us to have dinner at her place."

"And you said no, right?"

"That would've been rude if I said no."

"I'm not going." Dior huffed.

"Yes, you are," Clyde replied calmly as they walked back

to the car.

"What did he say to you?"

"Who?" Dior replied.

"Her husband...Jozua."

"Nothing, he was showing his condolences."

"I don't trust him, I don't want you hanging around him."

"There you go with that controlling shit."

"I'm not being controlling, Dior. Anyway, are you coming back to my place?" Clyde asked as they were walking back to the car.

"No, just take me to my mother's. I just want to be by myself for right now, but thank you so much for being there for me; I needed the support," Dior said to Clyde and she leaned over and gently kissed him on the corner of his mouth.

"No problem, if you need me, just give me a call, and I'll be there," he replied with a half smile.

His old self wouldn't have asked Dior where she wanted to go; he would have just driven home not caring about her feelings, but he swore after losing Dior that he was going to work on his possessive ways. After dropping her off at her mother's house, Clyde got out the car and walked around the car to let her out. She smiled at the fact that he was still a gentleman. Extending his hand waiting for her to grab it, Dior got out the car, folding her arm into his as he walked her to the door.

"I'm so sorry for your loss, nobody should have to go through this pain."

"Thank you. Although I am very sad for her passing, I'm happy that she's in no more pain, you know?"

"Yeah, I understand. When my father died, it was a bitter sweet moment for me. Although my father was a hard ass and never showed any kinda emotion, I still loved him, and I found comfort in knowing that he wasn't in pain anymore also. He died in his sleep, and I wouldn't have had it any other way. I hope I die the same way he did."

In shock, Dior stood there staring at him with a questionable look on her face. He had never talked about his family, let alone father.

"What?" he questioned.

"Uhum...nothing. You just never shared stuff like this with me."

"Oh, I'm sorry; I need to get going, I have a meeting."

"You and these meetings; nothing has changed."

"Mi' amor, everything has changed, but anyway, I will check in with you later," he said kissing her on the neck before walking away. Later that night before bed, she got a text from her sister

DAJAH: I FORGOT TO MENTION TODAY, WE NEED TO BE AT THIS LAWYER'S OFFICE TOMORROW MORNING AROUND EIGHT TO GET THE READING OF ELEANOR'S WILL.

Later that night, Dior tossed and turned in her bed finding herself having a hard time sleeping. Kicking the blanket off her, she huffed and puffed in frustration. She ran her hand up and down on the other side of the bed in search of her phone. Turning it on, she sent Clyde a text.

12 A.M. HER: YOU STILL AWAKE?

12:10 A.M. CLYDE: YEA, WHAT YOU DOIN' UP?

12:11 A.M. DIOR: I CAN'T SLEEP; I GOT SO MUCH ON MY MIND. WANT TO COME OVER? I COULD USE SOME COMPANY RIGHT NOW.

12:30 A.M CLYDE: I CAN'T RIGHT NOW, I'M A LITTLE TIED UP WITH WORK. DRINK YOU SOME HOT TEA; THAT ALWAYS HELPS YOU TO GET SOME REST. I WILL CALL YOU IN THE MORNING.

Feeling some kind of way, Dior tossed her phone on top of the pillow that was beside her.

# 9

# DIOR

*S*lowly getting out of bed after having a hard time getting to sleep, Dior dragged herself out of bed and slowly walked towards the bathroom. An hour had passed, and she was finishing up on the last touches of the outfit she was wearing to the lawyer's office, wearing a pink pencil skirt with a floral white off the shoulder blouse.

Once she arrived at the lawyer's office, she parked the car while looking around for any other car, and that's when she noticed she was the first one there.

"Now I know she told me eight," Dior mumbled to herself taking out her phone to check to see if she had gotten a text back from Clyde. Feeling disappointed that he didn't reply, Dior powered her phone off and tossed it back into her purse. After ten minutes of sitting in her car, a Nissan pulled up and parked beside her. As they got out their vehicle, Dior was checking them out trying to see if it was the man that was going to do the will reading. He wore a tan sports jacket with a blue fitted dress shirt underneath.

"Hello, ma'am, are you here for the reading this morning?" he questioned as he stood beside her car door.

"Um, yes, I am."

"Okay, I'm going to be the one reading the will this morning, I am a little late. I don't see the other person that is supposed to be here with you, we can give them a little more time to get here; the traffic is pretty bad this morning." He informed Dior.

"Sure," Dior replied. Collecting her things, she got out of her car, locked it, and proceeded inside. Thirty minutes passed, and Dajah finally showed up, with Jozua tagging behind her. Without speaking to her sister, Dajah sat in the seat beside Dior.

"Are we waiting for anyone else?" Dajah snobbishly asked.

"No, we can start," the lawyer stated as he was getting a folder out of his briefcase. "I want to thank you, ladies, for showing up this early morning, especially the day after burying your mother. I will try to make this process as fast and painless as possible; if everyone is ready, I will begin." He took a moment and looked at the both of them as they shook their head letting him know they were ready.

*"I, Eleanor Gibson, in sound mind, the day of ..."*

"Get to the point, please, I don't have all day." Dajah snapped.

"Ahem, okay," the lawyer responded as he flipped the page.

*"I leave the house and two million dollars to my daughter Dior Gibson. I leave nothing to my daughter Dajah Adams due to the simple fact that she has always made it very clear that she will never need or wanted my help, and in that case, I have left everything to my baby girl, Dior."*

After the will was read, Dior sat there speechless; she looked over to Dajah and could see she was fuming. The veins on the side of her head started to pop out as her eyes began to turn red.

"Go figure, fucking bitch; it never fucking fails with her. You know what, she's right. I've never needed anything from her pathetic ass, she was never there for me anyway!" Dajah hissed as she got up from the chair

"How could you say that, Dajah? Mother has always been there for the both of us."

"Dior, just shut the fuck up, because you know nothing of what you say, so please just continue to do what you've always been best at, looking stupid." Dajah snapped as she walked out of the office.

Jozua looked back at Dior and could tell that she was hurt by what Dajah said. He wanted so badly to go over and console her but thought against it, so instead, he walked out the office.

~

## TWO MONTHS LATER...

*"Yes, girl, he appeared outta nowhere at my mama's funeral, don't ask me how he knew about it; I'm just glad he was there, because lord knows I wasn't in the right frame of mind."* Dior spent most of her morning on the phone with British.

*"S,o the two of you are back together? What about your boo, Jayvon?"* British questioned.

*"Bitch, that nigga got a whole wife at home; his name ain't even Jayvon."*

*"Word! How you find that out?"*

*"Long story short, he's married to my sister, bitch, and his real name is Jozua."*

*"Bitch, what! Oh, hell naw, you mean to tell me this nigga been laid up under you for almost a year with a wife at home, ya' sister! I bet that nigga knew all along who you were and didn't give a fuck."*

*"He insisted that he didn't know who I was, but shit, he knew he was fucking married though. I tell ya', these niggas out here ain't shit, British. Although Clyde and I are trying to work on our relationship, I ain't gotta worry about all that extra shit; he's a*

*different type of breed, that lying and cheating shit isn't in him. He might be controlling and shit, but he ain't ta cheat."*

"Mmhm, he's a man though; don't put shit past a man."

*Beep!*

"Hold on, girl, someon'se on the other line." Dior clicked over.

"Hello?"

*"What are you doing?"*

"Nothing, on the phone with British."

*"I thought we had that discussion about you talking to her."*

*"And I thought we had that conversation about you telling me who I can and cannot talk to."*

Clyde grunted and ran his hands over his perfectly placed hair.

*"That dinner at your sister's is tonight, I need you to go shopping and find you something nice. I left my black card in the bedroom on the dresser. Tony will drive you wherever you need to go. I will be home around six, so I expect you to be dressed and ready."*

*"I don't see why I need to attend this dinner tonight. You already know we don't get along, and I can't be under the same roof as her for too long."*

*"Because I need you there by my side tonight, so please, find you something beautiful for dinner tonight."*

"Ugh, I guess." Dior sassed before clicking back over to an impatiently waiting British.

*"Girl, I gotta go. Clyde has this dinner he needs to attend tonight and insists that I tag along."*

*"He needs something pretty on his arm, huh?"* British sarcastically replied.

*"Girl, bye."*

Hanging up the phone, Dior checked the time; it was already two. She had a few hours to find a dress and get her hair done. Dior dialed up a salon who specialized in natural hair; she set an appointment and headed towards the bathroom to get ready. Once she finished her bathroom routine, she slipped on a pair of jean shorts and a black tank top pairing them with some white platform sandals. She had thick four-c type hair that went down to the middle of her back when it was stretched. Most of the time, she had it up in a large puff or a protective style. Dior took the black card off the dresser and tucked it into her purse and headed downstairs to greet Tony.

"Hey, Tony," Dior greeted him with a warm smile.

"Hello, Ms. Dior, and how are you doing this afternoon?"

"I'm doing pretty good. You ready for some shopping?"

"Of course," Tony replied with a chuckle. Tony waited for her to get into the car before he shut the door.

"So, where to?" he asked looking at her in the rearview mirror.

"Um, I don't know. Clyde said something nice for dinner tonight. Do you know any place?"

Tony thought for a moment before nodding his head. He started up the engine and took off. Twenty minutes passed, and Tony was parking in front of a fashion store called Stanley Korshak. It was a place Dior never heard of; she worried that they wouldn't carry her size because she was thicker. Walking into the store, Dior could already feel the negative vibe, and just by looking around, she knew they wouldn't carry her size.

"Can I help you?" a pretty, petite, redheaded woman asked walking towards Dior, showing her pearly whites. Dior could tell that she had just gotten her teeth done; she could barely close her mouth all the way, and she had a slight lisp.

"Um, no, not right now; I'm just looking."

"Okay, my name is Kimberley, and if you need anything, I am right over there." Kimberley pointed towards the cash register. Dior nodded her head with a fake smile and continued her shopping. She walked around the store and looked at the clothes, and she knew she wouldn't be able to fit any of them, but she was determined to buy something out of that store. Dior went towards the shoes and picked out a couple of pair of heels and waved her hand to get Kimberley's attention.

"Yes, do you need help with something?

"Yes, I was wondering if you had these in a size eight?"

"Um, yes, we do, but don't you think they may be a little bit too expensive for you."

"Don't worry about what's in my pockets; worry about getting my shoes. Please, and thank you." She nodded her head with her lips tooted up. Dior didn't give a fuck how the bitch was feeling. Five minutes later, Kimberley walked out the back with a couple of boxes and sat them down in front of Dior. After trying on all the shoes, she decided to buy them all.

"I like all of them; I think I'ma buy them all" The woman popped her head up looking at Dior with a mysterious look.

"Um, okay, I will take them to the register for when you are ready."

"Thank you," Dior replied back while putting her sandals back on. Once Dior finished trying on damn near the whole shoe section, she was ready to check out. As the woman rung up Dior's things, she kept glancing over at Dior wondering how she was going to pay for everything. She already had the police department on speed dial in case she tried to run out of the store without paying.

"That's      four-thousand-seven-hundred-and-forty-five dollars," the cashier stated with a devilish grin. Without speaking a word, Dior got out the black card and handed it to the woman, grabbed her bags, and waited for her card.

"Just a little lesson, don't ever assume because a person looks like me that they don't have money; you don't know what a person has in their pockets. They could be your best customer, Ms. Kimberley."

After Dior schooled the woman, she walked out the store with her six bags in her hands, handed them to Tony to put in the trunk, and got in the car.

"Did you find everything you were looking for?"

"No, not really. I just spent a shit load of money to prove a fucking point though."

"Was there a problem in the store? Should I contact Mr. Night."

"No, I took care of it, they didn't have my size. Take me to Ashley Stewart; I know that store has everything that I need for tonight."

Tony nodded his head, started up the car, and headed towards their next destination. After she finished her shopping and getting her hair and nails done, she walked out to where a waiting Tony was. Making it home, she called out to Clyde to not get an answer. Taking out her phone, she dialed his number to see when he was arriving home. There was no answer, so she left a message, hung up, and headed up the steps with her bags in hand.

# DIOR

"*D*ior, are you ready?" An eager Clyde huffed as he walked towards the bedroom. Glancing at his watch, it was already five-thirty.

"Yes, I'm ready, just putting on my shoes!" she shouted back from the walk-in closet. After putting her heels on that she bought earlier that day, she looked herself over in the full-length mirror and just loved how everything came together.

～

ONCE THEY ARRIVED AT THE HOUSE, Tony parked the car and got out and opened the door for Clyde, while Dior waited for her door to be opened. She got out her compact mirror to check her hair and makeup once more.

"You look ravishing." Clyde assured her as he extended his hand for her to take it. She slowly stepped out the car, fixing her dress, and she looked over to Clyde brushing her hand across his hair fixing the piece of hair that was out of place. He smiled and kissed her on the lips. "You know how much I love you," he softly said, grabbing her by the hand.

"No, why don't you tell me."

"How about I show you tonight after dinner? Now come on, we're already an hour late," Clyde said, leading Dior to the door. He rung the doorbell.

"I hope Dajah is in a good mood tonight," an anxious Dior stated as they both stood there waiting for someone to answer.

"Everything will be fine, love, and you look beautiful."

She looked up at Clyde and smiled. Just by his comment alone, her butterflies felt at ease. She glided her hands down her dress once more making sure it was perfect. The door opened, and the butterflies were present again. Dajah stood there staring at her sister for a moment before she spoke.

"Can we come in?" Clyde asked with a vague look on his face. They both stepped into the grand entranceway, and Dior was stunned by how beautiful Dajah's home was. She had never seen such tall ceilings and gorgeous crown moldings. The foyer was spacious with a double circular staircase with an elegant chandelier, which swayed between the stairs. The home looked extremely expensive; she was afraid to touch anything in fear of breaking something.

"It's so nice to have you in my home tonight, Mr. Night. It still takes some getting used to, seeing my sister with my boss. I guess it's true when they say the world is such a small place," Dajah said with a nervous chuckle.

While Clyde and Dajah talked, Dior looked over and saw Jozua walking towards them, and immediately, she knew her night was going to be everything but okay.

"Mr. Night, you met my husband, Jozua at the funeral." Without a reply, Clyde nodded his head in agreement.

"Let's go into the entertainment area," Dajah said

walking towards the room, and the three of them followed suit.

"I am so happy that I'm finally able to meet the man behind it all. When you agreed to have dinner at my house, I was so euphoric. Everything had to be perfect, so of course, I hired one of the best celebrity chefs and the best waiters."

While Dajah was speaking, a waiter came into the living room with a gold tray in his hand and glasses filled with the most extravagant champagne. Everyone grabbed their glasses, and Dajah raised hers in the air and waited for everyone to follow suit.

"First, I would like to thank you, Mr. Night, for gracing me with your presence tonight, and I'm genuinely appreciative. Also, for bringing my sister. Although we have many differences and have not always seen eye-to-eye on certain things, I am delighted that she came, even though I had no idea the boyfriend she had been speaking on was my boss, so cheers." Everyone clinked their glasses and took a sip.

"These are beautiful wine glasses, Dajah. Where did you get them?" Dior asked, taking another sip of the champagne.

"Ha-ha, foolish sister, these are not wine glasses. These are more expensive than some basic wine glasses. They probably cost more than that dress you're wearing right now. These are called champagne flutes, but of course, you wouldn't know anything about that, but to answer your question, they were wedding gifts actually from a good friend of ours. She knew my taste is nothing but exquisite and knew I wouldn't accept anything but the best."

"Mr. Night—"

"You can call me Clyde," he interrupted.

"Okay, Clyde. Did you know my sister came into some

money? Eleanor left her two million dollars along with our childhood home.

"Not now, Dajah."

"I mean, that's your man; shouldn't he know that Eleanor thought you needed the money more than I did? Since you were the child to not be as successful as I."

"Dajah, I said not now. If you're feeling some type of way about it, then we can discuss it at a later time."

"Feeling some type way, psshht...never. Why would I feel a certain way when I have my own? I've never needed Eleanor to save me or provide for me. Even when we were little, I made a way to get what I wanted."

"Dajah, leave Dior alone," Jozua interrupted Dajah rant.

"What, I'm not doing anything, or hurting anyone's feelings, am I, and anyway, why are you taking up for her?"

"I'm not taking up for anyone; I'm just tired of hearing you bitch. Besides, when is dinner gonna be ready?" Jozua said, pouring himself a third glass of champagne. He was tired of seeing this man's arms wrapped around the woman he wanted to spend the rest of his life with.

Dior stood there with a smile on her face as Clyde whispered in her ear. Seeing them together made him sick. As Dajah put her attention towards her husband, she suddenly heard the worst sound of her life--the sound of her delicate champagne glasses fragmenting into pieces. She looked over and saw her sister standing there with a dumb look on her face. "Oh, I am so sorry, Dajah. I know how much these meant to you. I don't know what happened; the glass just suddenly slipped out of my hand. I'm so sorry," Dior apologized, but Dajah knew better. She knew her sister had every intent on destroying her things. *That's why I never invite you to my home because you're always destroying shit,* Dajah thought to herself as she snapped her fingers for a waiter to clean up the mess.

"I will replace it." Clyde volunteered as he kneeled down to help the waiter pick up the broken pieces.

"No need, and please, you shouldn't be helping the help. I'm sure they can manage." Clyde got up from his knees and put the broken glass in the trash can beside him. He fixed his suit, glimpsed at his watch, and noticed that it was already ten in the evening. He needed to get out of there soon; he had some other business to attend at one of his whore houses.

"Are you okay?" Clyde questioned.

"Yes, I'm alright."

"Good, now go to the bathroom."

Just by the tone of his voice, it made her nipples instantly erect. She knew what he wanted, and she wanted to give it to him

"Dajah, where is your bathroom?" Dior inquired, looking around the home. The last time she remembered being at her sister's house was when Dajah was living in apartments. She felt like she had missed so much of her sister's life. First, her marriage, now a new home. Although Dior felt proud of her sister, she also felt a little envious of her. She had always wondered when she was going to have that life. A husband, a nice career, and maybe even some kids. She had often wondered if Clyde had ever thought about wanting children. In the four years that they have been together, that was a conversation they never had. Dajah angrily pointed in the direction of the bathroom. Dior rolled her eyes and walked towards the direction she pointed in. As she walked around Dajah's home, she started taking in how beautiful her home was. Dajah's home was like a mini-mansion, the interior of the house was a lot more sticking than the external appearance.

She ran her middle finger along the cream walls until she came upon a door. Opening the door, it was the bathroom. It was small but nicely decorated; everything on the walls were teal with a little black mixed.

She turned the water on and allowed the warm water to run through her hands.

*Knock! Knock!*

There was a soft tap at the door. Dior turned the water off. "Give me a minute!" she said, but the little tap continued. Rolling her eyes, she unlocked and slowly opened the door only to be pushed back inside.

"You smell good tonight, and this dress you're wearing, is distracting me from doing business."

"I'm sorry, I didn't mean to distract you," Dior responded with a smile."

"Don't be sorry; you're beautiful as you always are," he said, brushing himself up against her as he put his large hands around her neck.

"Clyde, what are you doing?"

"What, did I tell you about questioning me?" he said in a soft but stern tone. He shoved her up against the wall, spread her legs, slipping his fingers between Dior's thighs.

"No panties, I see, just how I like it."

Dior bit down hard on her bottom lip to keep from crying out in bliss. She loved the way he made her body feel every time he touched her. An electric surge went through her like a tree that had been struck by lightning. He took complete control of her; Clyde wrapped his masculine arms around her waist and lifted her up off the floor, pressing his

lips up against hers as he kissed her deeply and passionately, and at that moment, nothing mattered. She didn't care
that she was in her sister's bathroom on top of her sink
being fingered.

"I see how your sister's husband has been looking at you
tonight, was there anything between the two of you?"

Dior searched for the answer to give him; she knew how
controlling he was, and if she said yes, he could likely go out
there like a caveman and bash his head in, or he could
completely understand the whole deal.

*Why not just come clean about it? I mean, it's not like you
guys were together at the time, so you weren't cheating on him,*
she thought to herself before coming up with an answer

"No, there was nothing between us, I don't know why
he's been staring at me all night. Speaking of sister, I see
how she's been looking at you the whole night, so I should
be asking you the same question. I mean, you've never told
me that my sister was working for you."

"How was I supposed to know she was your sister? And,
your sister isn't my type, and even if she was, I got what I
want right here in front of me. Don't you ever forget that you
belong to me," he stated as he continued to run his finger
around her clit. His voice was so thick and full of lust, Dior's
heart began to beat rapidly as if it was trying to escape her
chest. Her legs started to shake as she could feel herself
about to explode. Her moans were beginning to get louder;
Clyde muffled her cries with his lips. He bit down on her
bottom lip as his finger still invaded her body.

"Dior, are you alright in there? You have been in there
for a while now. Is your stomach messing with you? I
remember when we were little girls you seemed to always
get constipated? If so, I got some stool softeners in the cabi-
net!" Dajah shouted loud enough for the whole damn

neighborhood to hear, but Dior herd nothing. She was too consumed by Clyde.

"Your sister, is um...very interesting."

"Yea, I know; she's a blast to be around," Dior sarcastically replied.

"Ha-ha, well, we will finish where we left off later," he said taking his finger out of her box, putting them into his mouth.

"We better get back," Dior said fixing her dress. Heading out of the bathroom closing the door behind her, she noticed Jozua standing up against the wall looking at her.

"What?" she nonchalantly said while passing him by. He grabbed her arm.

"I want to see you tonight," he said in a slur.

"You should go to your wife. Now let me go," Dior demanded, yanking her arm from his grip. He leapt towards her, blocking her from walking any further and grabbing ahold of her again.

"Take your hands off her." Clyde snarled, standing behind him. His beautiful, soft eyes were now deep and sinister like.

"Is everything okay?" Dajah questioned, looking at the three of them.

"Yea...yea, everything is fine. I was coming to see if Dior was okay," Jozua said, fixing his shirt.

"Okay, well, dinner is ready," Dajah said, grabbing ahold of Jozua's arm.

"I don't want to see him putting his hands on you again. Whatever you had with him, ends," Clyde warned in his dominating tone before walking off, leaving Dior standing there alone. Dior hurried to catch up to him. "I already told you nothing was going on between us, Clyde," She said, walking in front of him stopping him in his tracks.

"Why must you lie to me, Dior? He looks at you the same way I look at you, so stop it," Clyde quietly said before moving her out of his way. Taking a deep breath, all she wanted was the night to end.

Everybody sat at the table and began to eat. Dior sat beside Clyde. Moving closer to him, she whispered in his ear, "I'm sorry." He looks at her and smiled, and his hand began to move up her thigh. Rubbing her inner thigh slowly, she slowly inched her legs apart, giving Clyde more access. Taking a sip of her champagne, Clyde reached over and moved a flyaway hair out of her face. She looked over in her sister's direction and noticed her staring at them with a stank expression.

"You never told me how the two of ya'll met?" Dajah questioned, while the servers brought more food.

"We met at the beach just when I moved to L.A. I was only there for a couple of weeks and decided to go to the beach on a Saturday. He asked me out for a couple of drinks, and two dates later, here we are."

"It only took two dates to get you to be with him? Dang, I swore mother taught us better than that. When Jozua and I first met at a business retreat, it took a few months before I gave him the time of day."

"A man like myself, I wouldn't have waited a month. I knew what I wanted, and I knew that she was everything I needed in my life, so there was no point in waiting months," Clyde casually said while taking a bit of his food."

He was starting to get sick of Dajah's low blows towards her sister. If only she knew how unattractive that shit made her seem.

*I should kidnap her and sell her to my lowest bidder. Her pussy is probably used up,* Clyde sat there pondering as he smiled and nodded his head. He was beginning to get bored with it all.

"Dior, what do you plan to do with mother's home? I assume you're not living in it since you're with Clyde."

"What do you mean, what do I plan to do with it? I plan on keeping it."

"What a waste. I will never understand why mother gave you the house, instead of giving it to me. You need to either rent it out or sell it, one or the other. Better yet, why don't you sell it to me, and I will take it off your hands."

"I'm not doing that, Dajah. Like I said earlier, we will talk about that later." Dior leaned over and kissed Clyde on the cheek.

"I'll be back," she said before getting up from her seat making her way to the kitchen where the servers and chef were hanging out. Taking a glass off the counter, she went into the fridge to get another bottle of champagne. Pouring her another glass filling it to the rim, Dior took a couple of big gulps. Hearing foots steps approaching the kitchen, she knew it was her sister just by the sound of her heels hitting the marble floor.

"What do you think you're doing?" she asked, standing in front of Dior with her arms folded.

"What do you mean? I'm getting some wine; I'm sorry, I mean champagne."

"You're acting like a dimwit; you know what the fuck I mean. Why are you with him, with Clyde?"

"I'm doing no such thing, and it's none of your business what I do or who I decide to be with."

"It is my business when it has to do with my pockets." Finishing the glass of champagne, Dior poured herself another.

"You think you can come in my home with this, *I'm better*

*than you* attitude, just because you're dating a billionaire? Trust me when I tell you, that men like him will never have a girl like you as a wife."

"And what is that supposed to mean, girl like me? The fuck."

"I know you've heard the word basic; that's you, just some poor little girl trying to live this lavish lifestyle, but sis, no matter what he dresses you in or how much money he throws at you, you will always be simple, always be that poor girl that needs mommy's attention."

Feeling the urge to punch Dajah in the throat, she decided against it. Instead, she grabbed her a bottle and began to walk back to the table. Before she could leave out, Dajah grabbed her by the arm, digging her nails into her skin.

"Dajah, get your hand off of me." Dior fumed.

"You think because you're pretty, you can have any man you want, but let me tell you something, Dior, you're not. You're nothing, Clyde will never want a fat, dark bitch like you in his life. Women like you, he will use and throw away when he gets bored and is ready for a real woman."

"Why are you so worried about what I got going on, Dajah? You're the one that grew up with every damn thing. You never had to go to school wearing hand me downs. You were the homecoming queen and father's favorite. When you left for college, I had to live in the shadows of the popular Dajah; I was never good enough for neither mother nor father, but now, big sister," Dior continued, snatching her arm from Dajah's claws. "It's time for me to shine. I've done something that you never could do. I've caught me a big fish, and it seems like to me you're just a wee bit jealous that this big fish is more interested in this black, fat bitch than he is of Miss. Homecoming Queen." Dior sassed, walking out of the kitchen and going back to the dining area. She sat down a little too fast and became lightheaded.

"Is everything okay?" Clyde asked, putting his arm around her.

"Yes, baby, I think I drank too much," she said, but he knew something was bothering her. He made a mental note to ask her again in the morning.

"So, Clyde, can I call you that?" Jozua said, breaking the silence.

"Sure."

"How long are you going to be in Dallas?"

"Until I finish my business," Clyde replied.

"Are you married?" Jozua continued questioning.

"No, I've never married. I never really had time to do all of that, but maybe someday," he said, looking over at Dior.

"Hmm...so where are you from?"

"Europe, I was born there, but when I was five, my parents moved to America."

As Clyde was answering Jozua's questions, Dior looked over at Clyde stunned. Out of the four years they had been together, she never knew that he was born in Europe. *Shit, what else don't I know about this man?* Dior thought to herself.

"So, do you have any kids? I sense since you never married, you never had children, correct?"

For a second, Clyde paused, "No, I have no children. I've always been too busy to even think about having a family."

"So, what makes you think you have time for Dior?"

"Jozua, why are you so worried about what's going on in my life? Best believe he gives me all the time and attention that I need; I don't need you questioning my man about shit."

"Where is Dajah? It's getting late, and we need to discuss some business before we leave," Clyde said, getting up from the table, looking back and forth between Dior and Jozua. He didn't want to leave her here with him, but there was business to be handled, and since Dior was clearly checking him, Clyde felt certain that she wouldn't let him further mess with her.

"She's in her office," Jozua replied.

Clyde left out of the dining area and headed towards Dajah's office; he remembered where it was from earlier when she showed him around the home.

"So, you must be into this nigga since you stickin' up for him and shit?"

"He is my man, Jozua, so why wouldn't I stick up for him, and besides, it's none of your business what goes on between us."

"What all do you know about this man, Dior?"

"I know enough."

"How far have you gone into his business? I mean, what other things does he do besides real estate?"

"He does nothing else, why?"

"Nothing, just wondering."

Jozua got up from where he was sitting and sat beside her. He reached under the table, and placed his hand on her thigh, moving his hand upward until he was close to her pussy.

"Come here," he demanded, pulling her closer to him.

"Why don't you go to your mother's house, and I can drop by tonight. I've been missing that good-good," He said as he leaned into her.

"I'm not doing this, Jozua."

"Doing what?"

"Fucking this... Us...what we had is over, dead, no more."

"What we had will never be over, Dior."

"The day I saw you with my sister and found out that

y'all were married, is the day we ended. Now, let me go; I need some air," Dior said. Getting up from the table, she stumbled a little.

"Whew, I think I've had a bit too much to drink tonight," she said out loud to herself. Jozua grabbed her by the arm and yanked her back down. She lost her balance and almost fell on the floor before he caught her and guided her to the seat.

"You're acting different since this Clyde person has stepped into your life, but remember, that white piece of shit can't please you and do for you the way I can, I know he doesn't give you the kind of attention that I gave you."

"Jozua, if you don't get up out my face right now, I will shove this bottle down your throat."

"I have wonderful news," Dajah said, startling both Jozua and Dior. Jozua eased his grip, getting up from the table.

"I am now a partner of Night Real Estate Corporations," she said, chipperly.

"Oh, that's wonderful," Dior replied, looking at Clyde, to only notice that he wasn't smiling. Coldness had seeped into his eyes. Dior knew he saw Jozua's hands on her. Getting up from the table, Dior made her way to the front door.

"Where are you going?" Jozua asked as he ran after her.

"Let her go, Jozua. We're about to have dessert." Dajah stopped him

"I will also be going to New York in a couple of days to close some deals. I will be gone for a few months," Dior heard Dajah cheerfully announce as she closed the front door. Walking down the steps, she allowed the cool breeze to brush up against her face.

"Penny for your thoughts?" a voice said, startling her. Turning around, it was Clyde standing there with those beautiful blue eyes sparkling under the moon. Looking at him, Dior found herself falling in love with him all over.

"Oh, I don't know, just thinking."

"What are you thinking about, Bubbles?" Dior couldn't help but smile when he called her by the nickname he gave her. The first time he saw her naked, the first thing that came out of his mouth was bubbles. She looked at him with a *what the fuck* expression, and all he did was smile.

*"Your ass is perfectly round like a bubble is all,"* he replied with a devilish grin, that was then, and she'd since fallen in love with him calling her that.

"Bubbles, what's bothering you?" he asked again, snapping her back to reality.

"Nothing important, I just needed to get out of that house for a while. I can only be around my sister for so long."

"Come here," he said, pulling her into him. He stood there with so much confidence and power. She slowly walked towards him and allowed him to wrap his rippling muscles around her. Feeling his massive chest up against her breasts, he made her squirm, as her body reacted to his in ways that were unexplainable. She took in a deep breath smelling his scent; she couldn't deny it any longer. She wanted to be his wife; she wanted to belong to him forever.

"Clyde?"

"Yeah?"

"Have you ever really thought about marriage?"

"I don't know, not really. Why? Is that something you want?"

"I don't know, maybe someday."

"I don't know, Bubbles. Marriage is a different ball game, I've seen marriages go from gold to shit in months, my parents didn't have such a great marriage."

"Why don't you ever talk about your parents?"

"Because I didn't have such a great childhood is why."

Dior didn't question him anymore; she let his answer be the end of it. *Was Jozua right? How much do I know about him? I don't want to play house; I want to be more, and I know I deserve more,* she thought to herself.

Taking his jacket off, he wrapped it around Dior's shivering body. He slowly moved his large hands inside of the jacket, and he pulled her in closer, planting his lips on top of hers. Sharing a kiss for what seemed to last a lifetime, his lips still held that magical touch. "You ready to go?" Clyde whispered, still holding onto her. Taking out his phone, he dialed Tony's number, letting him know that they were ready to leave.

"I'm going to say goodbye to your sister before leaving," he said, kissing her again. Not ready to go back inside, she stayed outside looking up at the stairs. Five minutes had passed, and she was beginning to get impatient. Going inside, she walked around the house until she stumbled upon the office, overhearing the conversation between Clyde and Dajah. She listens as her sister asked him what he saw in Dior and how she could benefit him more than her. Dior rolled her eyes and let herself be known.

"Thank you for inviting us, we had such a wonderful time, and congratulations on your promotion, but I think it's time for us to go home; it's getting late, and I need to put my man to bed," Dior said, taking Clyde by the arm and walking out.

Getting into the car, Dior was anticipating being home and laid up under him that night. They hadn't slept together in a few weeks now. With him being gone on business all the time, when she was sleeping, he was gone, and when he was sleeping, she was gone, so just being able to lay in the same bed that night was satisfying to her. The drive back to the house was quiet; they were both stuck in their thoughts. She looked over at him and wondered what he was thinking. The way Dajah acted that night made Dior feel some type of way, and she didn't understand why a woman who had everything could be so bitter and miserable.

No matter how many times Dior saw Clyde's home, she always got the same expression--she was in awe by how immaculate the home looked. The house was two-stories, five bedrooms, and three baths, with a two-car garage and an inside swimming pool with a hot tub attached, and it sat behind an intricate designed gates.

Tony stopped at the gates, rolled down his window, and pressed a few buttons and waited for the gates to automatically open. Driving up to the front door, the driver got out to let Clyde out first. He then got back into the car. Clyde walked over to Dior's side to let her out. Once they were inside, Dior immediately took her heels off and sat her bag on the table beside the front door. She went into the living room where he was slouched on the sofa with his hands over his eyes, not paying any attention to what she was doing.

Straddling him, she could feel his bulge up against her bare pussy. Leaning down, she kissed his lips softly. Clyde took his hands from around his face and pulled her in, kissing her ferociously. His lips felt like butter and tasted like strawberries. Sliding his hand up her dress, he pulled it over her head. His tongue slowly moved over her collarbone; she instantly melted into him. Cupping her breasts, he kissed and licked around her erect nipples. Dior's juices escaped her begging body, yearning for him to enter her to fill her up. He marked her body like he was marking his territory.

Unbuckling his pants, he slid himself inside of her wetness, drawing a sharp breath as he entered her.

"Fuck, you feel so good." He grunted as he slowly thrust his hips. Wanting to feel every inch of him inside of her, she closed her eyes as his thrusts came harder.

"Open your eyes." He softly commanded. Dior did as she was told. She looked into his eyes that were filled with so much lust and passion. He bit down on his bottom lip, placing both hands on both sides of her waist and fucked her faster. Lying her down on the couch, lifting up her leg, he put it over his shoulder, slamming his massive dick inside of her. She let out a wild screech like an animal, wrapping her arms around his neck leaning up against him. As she feels her passion rise, her body convulsed, and her legs started to shake uncontrollably. His last thrusts were deeper and harder. He let out a wild groan and released his love inside of her. Falling flat on top of her, she wrapped her arms around him. Kissing her neck and lips, he pulled out still breathing heavily. He wrapped his arms around her and held onto her tightly as if he was taking ownership of her.

# DAJAH ADAMS

*D*ajah was feeling more prosperous in the last few months, with being the only woman in Night Estate to have sold not only one, but four million-dollar homes. Being a partner in a dominating male business, she knew that she had to go above and beyond to prove herself not only to Clyde but to herself that she was the perfect fit for the company. When she'd initially tried to get a job with the company, she interviewed and realized her smarts and knowledge of the business wasn't going to be enough to get in the door, so she'd made a bid as a partner, but she hadn't heard anything back about it yet, but now, that Clyde was dating her sister, and he was Dajah's boss, she would be able to speak to the head honcho in charge and finish buying her way into the company, but even with money, she still had to make her presence known, and show that she was more than just another ditzy girl.

While doing a walk through on a home, she got a call from Clyde's assistant letting her know that she needed to be at a conference meeting in Chicago the next morning, since none of the bigger partners were going to attend. Once the walkthrough was finished, she gathered her things and headed towards her car. Sitting in her car, her mind drifted off to Dior, still having a hard time understanding what Clyde saw in Dior. Just seeing them interact with each other that night made her sick.

*If he were attracted to anyone, it should have been me. I mean, I am the one that is successful out of the two of us. I have my own home, car, and I bring money into his business, not to mention my body is banging. With a small stomach, sexy C-cup breasts, beautiful slim thighs, and a nice little ass. I know he couldn't resist a woman of my stature,* Dajah thought to herself as she started the engine to her Mercedes.

She was still in her feelings about the conversation she had with her sister. Calling Dajah a *daddy's girl* was an insult to her; their father did things to Dajah that no father should do to his little girl. A father should never go into his little girl's room and do sickening things to her. Dajah felt like Dior was special because he never touched Dior, and she could never figure out why, and to her, she figured that the reason she didn't care too much for her sister, was because she was treated like the princess. She was treated like she was the only child. Their father would take Dior to the park or even to the movies while he left Dajah at home and only showed her attention when he was sexually assaulting her, but the day he took his last breath was the best day of her life, thinking that things were about to change at home, to only have it get worse. A year after her father died, their mother started going out dating, bringing different men home every other week. Dajah felt like that was the time for her to spend with her children instead of chasing dick. At the age of fourteen, one of her mother's boyfriends thought it would be a good idea to go into her bedroom and take advantage of her. He would say, *"You shouldn't be flaunting your body around me like you're a grown woman, now you're gonna take this dick and shut the fuck up."* While she laid there waiting for him to finish, her hate for her mother grew. She didn't put blame on the man that raped her, she put it on her mother. She was supposed to protect her children. Instead, she was too worried about who was going to keep her bed warm. As she got older, people said she was cold-hearted and standoffish. Her husband would say the only thing that made her nut was money, and they were all right. Dajah was cold-hearted and would always be about her money. She believed the only way to keep from getting hurt was to keep folks at arm's reach, including her husband.

She was ready to go home and soak her tired body and maybe spend some quality time with her husband. Things between Jozua and Dajah had been a little rocky. Ever since the night of the dinner, he'd been distant, not wanting her to touch him. He even slept in the spare bedroom and showered in the guest bathroom. Not knowing what was bothering him, but knowing him, it was probably something petty.

"Jozua!" Dajah shouted.

Going upstairs to the bedroom, he was lying across the bed, flipping through channels. Dajah was disappointed in her husband, for not having aspirations. She married him not only because he would make her look good out in public but also because she knew he was going somewhere prominent. His construction business was getting off the ground, and he was bringing in some good money. It was something that he loved, but one day, he woke up, and just decided he wanted to quit his job, and now, all he did was lay around the house while Dajah brought in the money. She had supported him in everything that he had wanted to do, giving him cash without questioning him, and that alone had made her question herself and why she was willing to take care of a healthy, grown man.

"Hey, baby," Dajah greeted him, sitting her things down. She climbs into bed with him.

"Hey, how was work?" he asked, not taking his eyes off the television.

"It was good. I sold three houses today. I also have a conference to go to tomorrow in Chicago; I thought maybe you could come along. The meeting shouldn't last that long, probably about an hour or two, then after we could do some shopping and maybe have dinner before coming back."

"Hmm," was all he said.

"What is that supposed to mean?" she questioned, getting up off the bed. She walked towards the dresser to remove her jewelry.

"I didn't mean nothing by it."

"You meant something by it, or you wouldn't have said it. Look, if you don't wanna go, you don't have to. I just thought it would be a great one-day vacation for the both of us."

"You've been spending a lot of your time at that office lately."

"Of course, I have. I'm trying to build something for the both of us, and since you're not working, I have to put in extra time at work to pay these bills."

"What are you trying to say?"

"Just want I said. You don't do shit around here but lay up in this house all day, when you could be out there busting them streets in search of a job. Anyway, I don't have time for this. If you don't want to go with me, that's fine. I'm not going to beg you, so go right ahead and lay around like a lazy bum."

"You're not going anywhere." He sneered as he jumped off the bed and leapt towards her, wrapping his hands around her throat. Dajah was caught off guard by his actions.

"You hear me! So, call that Night cat and tell him thanks but no thanks." He snarled.

That's when she could smell liquor on his breath, and that's when it all made sense to her.

"Get your hands off of me." She demanded as she tried to remove his hand from around her throat.

He looked into Dajah's eyes and could see how frightened she was, so he then slowly let her go. Falling to the ground, she began to suck in as much air as she could like she was taking her first breath.

"I expect you to do what I said." He demanded, walking out the room.

"Stop right there. Don't you ever in your life put your hands on me, do you hear me? I might have been good to you these past five years, but I'll be damned if I allow you to treat me like this!" she spat.

Getting up off the floor, she walked into the bathroom shutting the door. Going towards the mirror, she looked herself over not understanding what had gotten into him. He reminded her of their father when he would get drunk and use their mother as a punching bag. Shit like that, Dior didn't know about or chose to block from her memory. When her mother felt bad about the shit, she would shower Dajah with new clothes, new toys, and whatever she wanted to try and mask the shit that was going on at home, but unlike their father, Jozua hadn't always been that way.

The man that she married was kind, loving, and nurturing; she married a strong, independent man that stayed up late nights, taking care of business, but now, shit, he was a poor excuse of a man. Looking herself over in the mirror to make sure he didn't leave a mark, he was lucky she wasn't the type to bruise easily. Cutting on the shower, she stepped in letting the hot water run. Although she had to get up early the next day to leave, she couldn't stand being in the same house with him, so instead, she picked up a couple of fits for Chicago. Going into her large, walk-in closet, she tried to make up her mind on what she wanted to wear to the conference. Looking at her watch, she realized that it was still early, and that's when she made plans to go out and have a couple of drinks.

Dajah picked out a mini navy floral low V-neck lace bodycon, her slim five-foot-inch body frame looked sexy in it. Slipping on a pair of chunky blue heels, she grabbed her diamond clutch bag and headed out the door. Getting into her Nissan Patrol SUV, she was ready to see what kind of trouble she could get into for one night. Heading towards a bar that was also owned by Clyde which he named B&J Blues & Jazz Lounge, it was one of the most popular lounges. They were well known for their live bands. Entering the club, she took a seat at one of the booths. A waitress with long, dark hair, slim with large breasts, wearing black slacks and a black blazer came and took down her order. After ordering her three shots of Patrón and a Cesar salad, worried about keeping her figure snatched, she always said how she didn't want to end up looking like her sister-- a fat slob. To most men, she was beautiful with her dark skin, wide hips, and thick thighs, but to Dajah, she always thought she looked disgusting. After her food and drinks arrived, she sat in the booth alone and ate in peace.

"Look who decided to come out and play," a guy said. Looking up, it was one of her old flings who she messed around with before marrying Jozua.

"Hey, it's been awhile since we've seen each other," she replied.

"Yes, you haven't changed, still as beautiful as ever," he responded, sitting down at her booth. "So, how's life been treating you?" he asked.

"Everything has been going pretty good. I work at a real estate agency now. I got married five years ago."

"That's good news. Well, I better go before your husband comes and stomps my brains out," he said with a chuckle.

"Ain't nobody gonna be stomping your brains out," Dajah replied with a giggle. "So, sit your fine ass back down."

"So, where is your husband then?"

"Shit, I left his ass at home. He didn't want to come with me tonight, so I said fuck it. I'll go out alone."

"That's the Dajah I remember," he said with a laugh. Spending the rest of the evening drinking shots and dancing to the music, she couldn't remember the last time she had such a good time. After the tenth shot, she was good and buzzed, and so was Pablo.

"So would your husband be upset if you went back to my place?" he asked, pressing his body up against hers.

He smelled good and looked even better. "What he doesn't know won't hurt him," she replied. Grabbing her clutch purse, they both headed out the door. Her body was crying out for some attention, and she was going to listen.

# 12

## DAJAH

*Wonk...Wonk...Wonk*! Her alarm on her phone went off waking her up.

"UGH! Just ten more minutes, please," she mumbled, covering her head with her blanket. Still drunk from the night before, she ended up not making it home until four that morning, knowing she had to be at the airport at seven.

With her head pounding, and her body aching, she was close to canceling everything but knew that wouldn't look good. Slowly, she drug herself out of bed, not remembering much of what happened the night before, but she did remember the good-looking Spanish man that served her body right. Any other time, she wouldn't have given him the time of day, but the shit Jozua pulled had her feeling some type of way. She grabbed her phone to look at the time--it was already six. Mr. Night had a private jet waiting for her, and she sure didn't want to keep the people waiting.

Dragging herself to the bathroom with her eyes barely open, Dajah quickly jumped in the shower to allow the cold water to wake her up. Jozua wasn't in bed when she woke up, and he wasn't there when she laid in it, but how could she not be surprised? They hadn't slept in the same bed going on two months now. Something in her was telling her that he was sleeping with someone else, but she couldn't worry about that; she had other things to do.

After the shower, she rushed over to her closet to find something to wear--putting on a pink Chiffon blouse and a pair of skinny black pants, and finishing her look with a pair of pink heels and some gold earrings and bracelet. Grabbing the luggage and purse, for a moment, she thought about going into the spare bedroom to say goodbye to Jozua, but quickly thought against it. She stepped outside, where a waiting limo sat and waited for her. The driver got out and helped her with her luggage. Getting into the limo, her phone buzzed. Checking the phone, it was Clyde.

CLYDE: *I HOPE YOU HAVE SAFE TRAVELS, AND I WILL SEE YOU WHEN YOU GET BACK.*

She smiled at the text message; she just wished that they were an item. She was willing to show him things that were unimaginable, but instead, he picked Dior, but she wasn't about to let that stop her.

DAJAH: *THANK YOU, MR. NIGHT. I WISH YOU COULD JOIN ME ON THIS TRIP, I'M SO NERVOUS.*

CLYDE: *PLEASE CALL ME CLYDE, AND DON'T BE NERVOUS; YOU WILL DO GREAT.*

Ending their text, she put the phone back into her purse, sat back into the leather seats, and closed her eyes until she made it to the private terminal. Getting out of the limo, she made her way towards the waiting jet; the only person that was on her mind was Clyde.

# 13

## CLYDE

*C*lyde pulled up to a two-story, brick house, after dropping Dior off. Everything inside of him wanted to stay to make sure that she was going to be okay, but sharing part of his personal life made him feel a little uncomfortable. He didn't know what made him do that; he had never shared any part of his life, and that's what happened when he was around Dior. His walls came down to where he was comfortable sharing personal things. Clyde stepped out of his candy red Benz and made his way up to the front door. Fixing his Giorgio Armani suit, he rang the doorbell. After a few seconds, he could hear footsteps getting closer to the door.

"Hello, Mr. Night. Mr. Ashwood is expecting you, he's in his office."

"Thank you, Lucinda."

She was one of Kelvin's loyal servants. She stepped to the side to allow him to walk in and closed the door behind him. As he walked to the office, he took a couple of deep breaths before he made his way inside.

"Look who decided to show up, and I thought you

weren't going to show today. I was about to call some people to do a little house visit."

"And that would have been the biggest mistake you've ever made," Clyde replied, taking a seat.

"Ha-ha." Kelvin chuckled.

"Well, let's get down to business. I'm sure you have other businesses to take care of today."

"How many workers have you killed this month?" Kelvin asked Clyde looking up from his tablet.

"Ten."

"Mm-hm, and have you found the one that ran off?"

"Nobody has run off."

"What about the one that got pregnant by her client?"

"Oh, her I'm handling that--my men are searching for her as we speak."

"I need you to keep me posted on that, I don't need these women thinking they can just up and run away when the client tells them to do something they don't like, so when you find her, I need you to make an example outta her."

"And what about the child?" Clyde asked.

"Do what you wish with the child. I need you to go to Cuba to personally pick up more women; they have already been handpicked, we just need you to pick them up. There will be a cargo waiting for you to load them onto," Kelvin instructed.

"When?" Clyde asked.

"Tonight."

"Tonight?"

"Yes, is that going to be a problem?" Kelvin questioned.

"No, of course not."

"Good. One other thing, we are holding an event next month with some of the richest men from Texas and India, and I will need you there to stand in my place. I won't be able to attend."

Without replying, Clyde just nodded his head.

"Is there anything you want to add?"

"I'm thinking about leaving the business," Clyde randomly stated.

"Ha-ha." Kelvin chuckled. "Just when things are about to get interesting? You can't just leave when you feel like leaving, Mr. Night. I thought I made that very clear when you joined us."

"I'm getting too old for this shit. It was fun while it lasted, but I think I'm ready to move on to better things."

"There is no moving on to fucking better things, Clyde. Do I need to refresh your memory on what will happen if you just up and left?"

"I've seen that pretty, little chocolate thing you've been spending a lot of your time with. Maybe I should bring her into the business to keep you focused," Kelvin stated.

"Leave her out of it, Kelvin."

"Mmhm," was all he said. Something told Clyde that Kelvin was done with that conversation; it wasn't like him to just drop a subject, especially when he had eyes for something fresh.

"Oh, before I forget, there's an auction in Moscow that I need you to attend in two months. Gabino will be escorting you, and I expect you to be on that plane with him. Now, you can go!" He barked his orders, picked up his phone, and started handling business like Clyde wasn't even there

Walking out of his office, Clyde felt more frustrated than before he walked in the office. Lucinda escorted him out the house, and he made his way to his car and speed off. *How am I going to tell Dior about my past and about my future? Losing her isn't an option, but hiding this from her is eating me alive,* Clyde thought to himself as he drove down the highway.

Clyde stood in the dark corner of the warehouse while he watched his men beat this old man with the butt of their pistol. He held up his hand signaling for them to stop.

"All you have to do is tell me where your daughter is, and they will stop," Clyde questioned, for the hundredth time. He was beginning to get very annoyed with the man. The women that worked for him knew the rules; they knew who they belonged to, and running away not only cost him money, but also cost them their lives, and if need be, their family's lives.

"Fuck you! You evil son of a bitch." The old man hissed, spitting out a wad of blood.

"Suit yourself," Clyde calmly responded, lifting his hand for the men to continue. As he turned to walk out the warehouse, all that could be heard was the sound of fists hitting his flesh. Walking out of the building, he went directly to his car getting into the backseat. He took out his cellphone to check for missed calls. He saw that he had two missed text messages from his man at one of his whore houses, making a mental note to drive by their before making his way home.

He was ready to be home and under Dior; he had thought about telling Dior what he did for a living besides his business, but he was too afraid of Dior leaving him again. Afraid of what he would do if she decided to leave; he decided not to tell her. Clyde ran his hand slowly down his face in vexation.

"All the fucking old man had to do was tell me where his daughter was--that's all he had to do, but he was too stubborn to give up information," Clyde angrily mumbled to himself.

A week ago, while he was home laid up under Dior, he got a phone call alerting him that one of his girls ended up pregnant by one of her regulars. His whores understood that all pregnancies would end in abortion. He provided birth control and also monthly pregnancy tests; there would be serious consequences for those that refused to take them. Every two months, he also provided them with STD and HIV testing. Women who ended up with incurable diseases would be killed. If it was curable, he'd pass out some antibiotics and send her back to work. She'd be restricted to only sucking dick.

She knew the consequences of getting pregnant by a client, so she took his money and left with the client. She was Clyde's property, and he wanted his property back. After he picked the women for his whorehouse, they were thoroughly cleaned and branded like bulls, then moved into one of the many transitioning homes where they were broken in. Some of the women that came into the business easily transitioned, and some took a little more hands on to break in. This year was a special year. Word on the streets were that Russia had a virgin, and all the pimps, madams, and slave owners would be attending. Virgins in this business could make you a lot of money and surprisingly, they were hard to find and even harder to acquire. With the amount of money they brought in, they didn't go to the transitioning home; they were treated with more care. They were treated like fine wine, just until the pussy began to wear out.

That night before going home, he had to stop by the whorehouses to make sure everything was running the way things needed to be ran. Clyde walked through the dirty halls listening to the groans and moans of the men as the women pleased them. He could also hear a couple of women whimpering. Some of the men that came through wanted to indulge in something a little more dangerous. Those men paid a lot more to fulfill their hunger and fantasy.

"You need to put a handle on that hoe." One of the clients spat as he walked out of a room with a scratch mark on his face.

"What happened, sir?" Clyde asked.

"That bitch scratched me. I wanted to stick my dick in her ass, and she scratched me."

Clyde couldn't help but to chuckle on the inside at the way the man carried on. He thought he was about to break down and cry, but Clyde knew he couldn't have his hoes acting out.

"My apologies, sir. Would you like to pick one of our newer girls? They aren't as feisty."

"I'll come back later," he said with his handkerchief covering his little scratch. Going into the bedroom where he was, Clyde stood there in the door. Taking a deep breath, he knew what needed to be done.

"P-Please, Mr. Night, I won't do it again, please. I'm sorry, I promise it won't happen again. I-I was just scared; that's all, I was scared. Please."

Her plead for mercy rung on deaf ears. Clyde took out his phone, made a phone call, said a few words, and left out the room.

"I need you to watch her until my men come to pick her up." He told one of the guards that stood out in the hallway.

"Yes, sir," was all the guard said before walking towards the room.

## 14

## JOZUA ADAMS

*I*t'd been three months since the funeral, and still, he just couldn't stop thinking about the strange man that Dior was hugged up with. He laid in the spare bedroom listening as Dajah stumbled coming in late, he wanted to go down there and get in her shit, but he honestly didn't give a fuck about what she was doing. Their marriage might have looked good on the outside, but on the inside, it was a complete fucked up mess. He had asked himself a million times why he said yes to her proposal. Shit, he didn't believe in the whole woman asking a man for his hand in marriage. Jozua was old fashioned and believed that it was a man's responsibility to take care of his woman and to ask her hand in marriage when the time was right. Marriage was a serious thing to him, so he didn't understand why he said yes; he clearly wasn't in love with her or even attracted to her--he just blamed it on the liquor. Who he really wanted was her sister, Dior. When he found out that Dior was in fact Dajah's sister, he knew that things between them were over. If only she had stayed in L.A like he told her to. His plan was to fly down to Dallas to file for divorce and ask

Dior to marry him, but all that turned to shit when Dior called him from the airport telling him she was in Texas.

Jozua picked up his phone and dialed Dior's number to only get voicemail. He couldn't stand the thought of that man touching her soft, beautiful body. The thought of it made him furious. After tossing and turning the remainder of that night, he finally dozed off with Dior on his mind and how he was going to win her heart back. Waking up to the sound of his phone ringing, he turned over and looks at the Caller ID. Not able to recognize the number, he quickly pressed the red button, threw the phone on the floor, rolled over, and dozed back to sleep. Thirty minutes later, the phone rung again. Feeling agitated, he answered it.

*"What's up?"* he answered in a husky but irritated tone.

*"Is this Jozua?"* some sexy, sounding female asked.

*"Yeah, this is him. Who dis?"* he responded but in a calm tone. The voice on the other line made him change his approach.

*"This is Sandra; we met at the gas station a few nights ago. You gave me your number and told me to call you."*

He tried to remember a girl named Sandra. There had been many nights where he had gone out to clubs and given his number to random females.

*"Oh, yeha, Sandra. My bad, it took me a minute. I got pretty fucked up that night."*

*"That's alright, sexy. I got a little fucked up myself,"* she replied with a giggle.

*"Hell yea, so what's up?"*

*"Nothing much, I was hoping you could keep me company today."*

*"Shit, what are you trying to get into, baby girl?"*

*"Whatever. I got some good Kush and don't want to smoke it all by myself."*

*"Aight shit, bet. How about I go and pick you up, and we could come back to my spot and chill.*

*"Sounds like a plan,"* she replied, giving him her address. *"Aight, give me an hour. I need to finish up some work before I can play,"* he lied.

After they said their goodbyes, Jozua hopped out of bed feeling energized. He knew Dajah wasn't going to be home for the remainder of the day--she has been spending a lot of her time at the office, almost as if the office was her new home. Jumping in the shower, he quickly let the water hit his body and rinsed himself off. Getting out the shower, Jozua grabbed his phone and text Sandra to let her know that he was on his way.

Once he made it to her house, she had luggage and shit waiting outside her home. *Fuck, what was she planning on doing, moving in?* Jozua only had plans for tonight; he didn't want her spending the night. Fuck, get high, then send her ass on her merry way.

"Hey shawty, what's all this?" Jozua asked getting out his car.

"I thought I would be staying a few days."

"Naw shawty, I can't allow that. You need to take all this and put it back inside. Here, let me help you." He grabbed her things and tossed them back inside of her home.

"Now, you ready to go?"

"Yea, I guess," she replied, sounding a little disappointed. *What the fuck made this bitch think she was gonna be staying at my crib for a few days? This bitch got bird brains, what the fuck?* he thought to himself as he got into the car and drove off. As he sat at the red light, she dug into her purse and got out a fat blunt. Jozua looked over and couldn't believe his eyes. It looked like she put a whole bag of weed in that one blunt. She lit it up and puffed it.

"I'm sorry, daddy, did you want a hit?" she asked as she continued to smoke.

"Yeah, let me get a hit off that bitch." Taking off her seat belt, she leaned over to Jozua and put the blunt up to his mouth so he could take a few hits. As he was smoking it, she began to nibble on his ear, kissing him on his neck.

"Damn baby, wait until we get to the house."

"Why?" she replied as she continued to nibble on his neck. She moved down and unbuttoned his jeans, slid her hand down, and pulled out his dick.

"Damn, girl."

"I just can't wait any longer," she replied, stuffing his dick into her mouth.

"Shit, well gone ahead, baby girl; take that monsta," he said, pushing her head down further.

# 15

# CLYDE

*S*liding into the back seat of his car, Tony closed the door and made his way around to the driver's side. Clyde ran his hands through his hair in frustration. He started to feel the pressure of his business--not being able to close a deal on a million-dollar house had him a little on edge. He leaned his head back onto the comfortable plush headrest, closing his eyes trying to relax until the vibration of his phone interrupted him. Taking it out of his suit jacket, Clyde checked to see who it was. Not in the mood to talk to the person on the other end, he pressed the end call button sending them directly to his voicemail.

"Tony, take me to the nearest jewelry store," he instructed. Tony nodded his head and headed towards a jewelry shop. Clyde knew that Dior loved diamonds, and when he was feeling stressed, he had a habit of splurging; it was therapeutic for him to spend money on his woman. Tony stopped in front of a jewelry store, let Clyde out, and waited beside the car.

"Hello, Mr. Night, it's so good to see you. What can we do for you today?" the salesman asked with a smile on his face.

He knew every time he saw Clyde, he was there to spend some money.

"Is there anything particular you're looking for, sir?"

"Something for my woman. She loves diamonds, maybe some sort of diamond necklace."

"Ahh, I have the perfect gift," the salesman said as he hurried behind the glass and took out a beautiful diamond heart necklace. "This here is called the Center of My Universe Pendant; it's a beautiful diamond necklace that's shaped like a heart with a pave halo setting."

"How much?"

"Ten-thousand, sir." Clyde took the necklace and looked at it for a few moments before deciding on if he wanted to purchase it or not.

"I'll take it, make sure you put it in a gift box."

"Yes, sir," the salesman said with a little bit too much excitement. After Clyde paid for the necklace, they said their goodbyes as he walked out the shop.

"Where to, sir?" Tony asked as they both positioned themselves in the car.

"The flower shop," Clyde responded while opening the necklace box and looking at the necklace once more. Tony stopped at the nearest flower shop. Clyde got out and went inside, picking out thirty-six yellow and white stemmed roses, and put them in a beautiful red vase. After paying, he headed back to the car. Heading home, he texted Dior letting her know that he was on his way home like he did on a regular, feeling like a middle school kid waiting on his crush to respond back. Ten minutes later, she text back.

DIOR: HEY BABY, OKAY I'LL SEE YOU WHEN YOU GET HOME. Ending the text and turning off the phone, he slid it back into his breast pocket.

After making it home, Tony parked the car in front of the house.

"I'll see you tomorrow morning, Tony," Clyde said before getting out of the car.

"See you then, sir," Tony replied, looking in the rearview with a smile.

He was a nice man. He was older than Clyde with a wife, four children, and eight grandchildren. Clyde grabbed the vase of flowers and box that had the necklace in it and headed up the stairs, opening the door to the smell of food — salmon to be exact. Salmon was one of his favorite dishes. Walking into the kitchen, he saw Dior bent over pulling the food out of the stove. She had on a sexy embroidered mesh lace nightgown with a side slit that went up her thigh. *Fuck, her body looks fucking amazing,* Clyde thought to himself. His dick jumped to attention just watching her make her way around the kitchen. He sat the flowers down on the shiny marble countertop and slowly walked over to her. She was so engulfed in her cooking that she didn't even notice that he was standing behind her. He gently placed his hand on her butt, cupping it, not realizing how much of a butt man he was until she was in his life, she jumped to his touch.

"Oh, you startled me," she said, placing the pan on the stove.

"I'm sorry, I couldn't help myself. You look so irresistible in that beautiful gown," he replied, running his hand down to her thigh. "Stop, I gotta get dinner on the table," she said playfully pushing his hand away.

"Dinner can wait," he replied, pulling her away from the stove. Turning her around, he picked her up, sitting her on the countertop. "Awe, are those for me?" she asked, looking over at the roses while he kissed her neck and cupped her breasts in his hand. "Yeah, those are for you, this is also for you. He said showing her the necklace box.

"What did you do?" she questioned with anticipation.

"I didn't do anything, I thought this would look beautiful around your neck. Now, are you going to open it or what?"

She took the box and slowly opened it; he stood there waiting to see the expression on her face.

Dior gasped when she saw the diamond necklace. "Clyde, it's beautiful," she said as a tear randomly streamed down her cheek.

"Why are you crying?" he asked as he brushed the tear from her cheek.

"You have done so much for me, and I have done nothing for you."

"Mon amour *(my love,)* you have done so much for me. Just being here is more than enough, gracing me with your beauty every morning is all I ask," he said as he took the necklace and wrapped it around her neck. Once he clasped it, he brushed his finger across her lips before he placed his on top of hers.

She wrapped her beautiful legs around his waist. Sliding her shoulder strap down her shoulders, he began to kiss her shoulder slowly. "Mmm," she moaned softly. Her moans alone did something to him. He ran his tongue up to her beautiful lips, parting them with his tongue, sucking her tongue deep into his mouth, kissing her deep and passionately. She ran her hands up his chest unbuttoning his shirt. Once she gets it unbuttoned, she slowly ran her hands up and down his bare chest. Her fingers were running around like she was in a maze. Running his hands through her hair, he lightly pulled it. Her head tilted back as he nibbled on her chin.

"You're so beautiful, Bubbles." Clyde groaned, spreading her legs further apart.

Gliding her gown up over her thigh, he pulled her to the edge of the counter, kissing her body, making his way down between her thighs.

"You smell so good," he said, spreading her essence with his tongue, lightly licking and kissing her pearl. She grabbed a hand full of his thick hair and pulled him in deeper. As her moans got louder, he continued to eat her pink pearl until she climaxed in his mouth--her juices running down his face. Unbuckling his pants, his erection was starting to feel uncomfortable; she slid her hands down in his briefs and began to stroke his rock-hard dick. Then, without saying a word, she slid off the countertop and got on her knees, taking his thickness into her mouth. Clyde tilted his head back, and all he could think about was how good her lips felt around his manhood. He pulled himself out of her mouth before he climaxed. They both laid on the floor, Dior straddled him, and slide his dick inside of her wetness, rocking her hips back and forth grinding on his dick. Running his hands up to her breasts, her nipples poked through her lace gown. He slid the gown up over her head, he leaned up, and slid her large nipples inside of his mouth. They spent the next hour making passionate love on the kitchen floor. She creamed all over him. The way her pussy tightened around his dick, he knew she had a few good orgasms. After they both climaxed together, she collapsed on top of him.

"That was nice," she said.

"Just nice?"

"It was fantastic," she replied with a laugh.

"Well, so much for dessert after dinner."

"Yeah, well you shouldn't have that gown on. You know

what your body does to me." Lying on the kitchen floor, his phone began to ring.

"Ugh, fuck!"

"Ignore it," she replied, kissing his neck.

"It's probably something important," he said, sliding her off him. She got up and went over to the stove to put the salmon back into the stove to warm it up.

*"Hello, this is Night,"* he answered.

*"Yeah, I told you I wasn't interested,"* he said getting agitated

*"You know what happens when things don't go my way,"* the person on the other end said.

*"I'll be by there tomorrow then,"* Clyde replied and hung up.

"Who was that? It sounded important."

"It wasn't. The only thing that's important right now is you," he replied, grabbing her from behind and pressing her up against his naked body, his clothes were still lying on the floor.

"Stop it now. I'm starving. I don't know how many more times I can heat up this salmon before it dries out."

Waking up in the large California king size bed with Egyptian cotton satin sheets up against her naked body, Dior looked over to her left and saw Clyde still sleeping. He was breathtaking; he didn't have any noticeable stress lines around his mouth or eyes, and she couldn't help but smile at the thought of how innocent he looked, but she knew he was everything but. Dior's stomach started to grumble. Slowly sliding out of bed being careful not to wake him, she slipped on one of Clyde's shirts and made her way down to the kitchen, roaming through the fridge in search of something to eat.

"You're just going to stand there and let all the cold air out?" he asked, standing their butt naked.

"Oh, sorry, I just don't know what I want to eat."

"Well, I want some French toast," he replied as he sat on the barstool. He sat naked watching her prepare to cook. Looking over at him, their eyes met.

"What are you looking at?" she asked.

"My woman," he replied back, catching her off guard with that statement. Although they had been together for such a long time, he still had that way to make blush.

"You know, you're going to make me fat."

"Well, you said you wanted French toast," she replied back. "And anyway, I like my men with a little meat on their bones."

"And I love my women with a lot of meat on hers."

After they ate, they made their way back upstairs to get back into bed and did everything but slept.

# 16

# DIOR

*I*t was still morning. She woke up needing to get out of bed and get her day started. Her body was aching from all the loving they both shared. Grabbing her phone from the nightstand, she looked at the time; it was pretty early, six in the morning. Going into the bathroom, she turned the water on filling up the Jacuzzi tub. She placed some sea salt to soak her body and girly parts, also adding some scented oils with honey and milk bubble bath. Sliding down into the water, she let out a deep sigh while sinking down into the deep Jacuzzi. Grabbing her phone, she turned on Pandora to the R&B 80's. The sea salt made her body feel just right. She was finally at a point where she was actually happy with things between Clyde and her. Out of the whole four years, she had never felt such a connection with him as she did at that moment. Closing her eyes, she ended up dozing off.

"You're going to stay in there all day?" Clyde asked, walking into the bathroom to take a piss.

"I haven't been in here that long," she replied.

"You've been in here for almost an hour now. Isn't the water getting cold?"

"Yea, a little," she replied, realizing that her fingers were actually looking like prunes.

"I guess I've been in this tub longer than I anticipated," she said as she began to get out the tube.

"What do you have planned today?" he asked.

"I don't know, I'm kind of getting tired of sitting around the house all the time. I think it's time for me to find some sort of job."

"Have you thought about what you're wanting to do?

"Yes, I still want to open my own bar, and I've also thought about opening a woman's shelter."

"Really? And how long have you thought about this?"

"I don't know, since L.A. That was really the whole reason for me going down there was to go to college and open a few businesses."

"Really? Why haven't you told me about this? You know I can give you the money and anything you need to get it started. I do own six properties. My name alone will get you everything you need."

"Yes, I know, and that's the reason I never told you. I wanted to do it alone. I don't want to throw your name around like that and have that being the only reason I got what I want."

"Hmm... okay. Well, how about I loan you the money?" he said.

After she rubbed lotion all over her body, she stood in front of the mirror and began combing her thick hair.

"And how am I supposed to pay this loan off?"

"By marrying me."

"What? I'm serious, Clyde. How am I supposed to pay back all that money?"

"Look, when your company gets to where it needs to be and money starts to come in successfully, that's when you can begin to pay me back a little at a time, and I was serious about marrying me." Dior stood there for a moment, confused, because if she remembered correctly, he said he didn't want to get married, but again, she ignored it.

"Are you sure, Clyde?"

"About you marrying me?"

"Ugh, no. About the loan, stay on topic."

"Oh, thought I was. Yes, I'm serious. I don't care about giving you... I mean, loaning you a few thousand or whatever you need for the business, so no need to worry about finding you some slum job; you can get with one of my realtors, and they will help you with searching for the perfect spot," he replied, turning the shower water off and stepping out.

"Now I really must be getting dressed so that I can get out of here. I'm leaving Tony here to drive you around where ever you need to go."

After Clyde got dressed, he kissed her goodbye and left. She dressed in something simple, a t-shirt and some jeans. Going downstairs, she grabbed her mac pro laptop and went into the kitchen in search of the perfect property for her bar.

*"These parties are so fucking boring, when are we going to spend time together? Granted, we are always together now, and you have involved me in a lot of your business related things, and I'm grateful for all that, I really am, but this shit is starting to get boring."* Dior pouted on the phone to Clyde during one of many morning phone conversations they had together.

"You're going, Dior. One of the most important people will be at this event, and I need you there with me."

"Why do I need to be there, Clyde? He ain't there to see me, he's gonna be there to see you tonight."

"I'm not hearing it, I didn't call you to argue. I called because I need you to get dressed and fly out to New York to try on a couple of evening gowns, Tony will assist you and take you straight to the hotel."

"You want me to just stop what I'm doing and fly out to New York because you said so?"

"What are you doing?"

She took a few moments to answer.

"That's what I thought, now stop being obstreperous," Clyde harshly replied.

*What the fuck does obstreperous mean?* Dior thought to herself as she rolled her eyes as if he could see her. After hanging up the phone, she googled the word *(noisy and difficult to control.)* Feeling some type of way, she started thinking of ways to get back at him for making her do something that she didn't want to do. She got dressed in a pair of high waist, eight-button, dark skinny jeans and a red off the shoulder ruffle top pairing them with pointed toe red heels. While flat ironing her hair, her phone rang.

"Hello," she said answering the phone.

"Hey, girl, what you doin'?" British asked

"Getting dressed."

"Oh, where you off to?"

"Clyde has a private jet waiting for me, I need to be in New York for this event he's making me go to."

"Word, so you high and mighty now ain't you, going to these fancy events and shit?"

"Shit, if I had a choice, I wouldn't be going to these events. I much rather stay at home and spend some TLC time with my man. What have you been doing with yourself?" Dior asked

"Girl, I been alright; I can't complain. My sugar daddy been keepin' me busy, taking me on these lavish trips and shit."

"Sounds like you've been living the good life. Shit, I would give anything to go on vacation, besides going to these events. I've been searching for property to open up a bar."

"Business woman now. Shit, pretty soon you won't have time for this basic ass bitch right here," British stated with a laugh.

"Nah, I'll always have time for my girl," Dior replied, ending their conversation. Dior hung up and continued packing. An hour passed, and she was ready to head to the private jet. She grabbed the keys to the house and put them in her purse and walked out the door with her luggage dragging behind her. Going outside to where Tony was waiting, he was standing beside a stunning black 2018 Lexus Rx Hybrid.

"Nice car, Tony," she said, going inside. Making herself comfortable, she ran her hands across the noble brown leather seats. Making it to the jet terminal where her private jet was waiting for her, after Tony parked the Lexus in front of the jet, Tony got out and walked around to let Dior out. They both stepped into the black with gold trimming jet. She was in awe by how stunning the inside of the jet was; it looked fit for a queen. After Tony and Dior got seated, the jet took off.

Once they landed in New York, she was excited due to the fact that she had never been to New York. Having her last sip of champagne before exiting the jet, she noticed a candy red Jaguar waiting for her. Tony opened the door; waiting for her to get in, she entered the car, and they drove off towards the hotel.

Once arriving at the Peninsula Hotel, walking inside the

glamorous hotel made her feel expensive and boujee. Sashaying towards the front desk, she gave them her name, and they immediately gave her the room key. Dior looked around the hotel while walking towards the elevator. Dior was memorized by how beautiful the building was. Taking out her phone, she decided to snap a couple of pictures and post them on Instagram for her followers to see.

As she entered her room, she was amazed by how big her hotel room was. Before Clyde, she had never been to a hotel such as the one she was in. Whenever she spent the night at a hotel, it was always at Motel 6. *This is far from Motel 6*, she said to herself as she sat her luggage down beside the door.

Walking around the room, she noticed that there were two parts: the living room and the bedroom, almost like a mini apartment. She went over to the bedroom, and that's when she saw a couple of evening gowns hanging on a rack. Surfing through the gowns, she couldn't make up her mind on which one to wear that evening; they were all too beautiful to just pick one.

While in the bathroom taking a quick shower, she heard a knock at the door. Stepping out the shower, she wrapped her white robe around her body and made her way to the door.

"Who is it?" she asked, before opening the door.

"I'm Tiffany, um…Mr. Night sent me to do your hair and makeup for the night!" the woman shouted through the door.

When Dior heard Clyde's name, she quickly opened the door and let the woman in.

"Hello, it's so nice to meet you," the stylist said reaching out to shake Dior's hand. After they both greeted each other, the stylist explained everything and took a moment to set up. While Dior was getting her hair and makeup done, she began to take a few more pictures for Instagram and titled them *When yo' man sets up your hair and makeup, living the glam life.*

Once she was finished with hair and makeup, she took a few moments to look herself over in the mirror. Her face was beat to the gods, and her hair was perfectly in place.

"Thank you so much; I love everything." Dior beamed as she continued to look herself over in the mirror. After the stylist left, she began to look through the gowns that were hanging on the rack. She chose a Zoey Grey evening gown. Dior slipped the white gown on and loved how the stretchy fabric hugged her curves; it had a beautiful high neckline with long illusion sleeves that were covered with intricate beads that were in a gorgeous design. She turned facing the mirror to check out the open back that had the same beading as her arms. She finished the outfit off with a pair of white, suede, crystal, embellished sandals with an ostrich feather tassel that dangled in the front. Dior stepped back to check herself out once more in the mirror; she was in love with the finished look. She grabbed her phone once more and began to snap pictures of herself in the gown. While taking the last picture, there was another knock on the door. She walked towards the door and opened it, and there he stood--her date for the evening. He was so handsome in his Tom Ford Windsor black tuxedo His six-four frame was hypnotizing.

"You're looking exquisite tonight, Ms. Gibson," he said reaching his hand out for her to place hers in his. They left the hotel room hand in hand looking like the rich power couple that they were.

"You look dazzling, Ms. Gibson," Tony said, helping her into the ice-white Rolls Royce.

"Why thank you, Tony." Getting into a car, she started to feel a bit nervous. Her palms began to sweat, and she started to feel warm.

"Nervous?" Clyde asked, looking over at her.

"Yes. A little."

"Don't be. You're beautiful, and everything will turn out great." He reassured her, taking his handkerchief out of his breast pocket and handing it to her to wipe her hands.

"Oh, before I forgot," he said, going into his pocket and taking out a white box and placing it in her lap.

"What is this?" she asked, picking the small box up looking at it strangely like it was of some foreign object.

"Just a little something. What's the point of being with a billionaire if you get none of the perks?" he said with a smile. "Now open it."

"Oh my," Dior said with her hands over her mouth. "Clyde, they are stunning," she shockingly said.

"I'm glad you like them. They were pretty expensive, but I wouldn't have it any other way when it comes to you. We're almost at the event, are you going to put them on?"

"Oh, yes of course." Dior took the four caret stud diamond earrings out of the box, and put them in her ear. Going into her clutch purse, she took out her compact to take a glance at the beautiful earrings that sat perfectly on her ears.

"How do they look?"

"Not as beautiful as you, Bubbles," he softly said as he leaned in to kiss her. Once they arrived at the Frick mansion, the red carpet was already laid out waiting for them to step out on it. Tony opened the door for Clyde, and Clyde opened the door for Dior, stepping out to bright lights and cameras flashing in their faces. All eyes were now on them. Dior wasn't used to that kind of attention. She then realized that it wasn't just any dinner.

"Just stay by my side," he whispered in her ear, placing his hand at the middle of her back.

"Mr. Night! Mr. Night!" someone shouted. Clyde stopped and turned around to the person that was shouting his name.

"Don't you look handsome tonight."

"Thank you," he replied, pulling Dior closer to him.

"And who is this lovely lady beside you?" the red-carpet reporter questioned.

"This is Ms. Dior Gibson," he replied.

"How lovely, and who are you wearing tonight, Ms. Gibson?"

"Zoey Grey," Dior replied, running her hands down her evening gown.

"Well, you look exquisite tonight," the reporter said.

"Thank you," Dior replied with a smile."

"Is this a new romance?" the reporter asked, getting a little more personal.

"He looked down at me with parted lips like he was going to say something, but nothing came out.

"It's whatever Ms. Gibson says it is," he finally replied.

"Well, Ms. Gibson is there something more between the two of you?"

"Yes, of course," Dior replied. The reporter smiled, and before she could ask another question, he dismissed her. They began to walking inside the building. Before they made their way inside, they were stopped a couple more times for pictures. Clyde wrapped his arm around Dior and smiled at the flashing lights. Once the pictures were over, they made their way inside the mansion. Stepping inside, all eyes were now on them.

"Clyde, so glad you could make it; we were starting to worry you weren't going to show," an older man said, walking up to them. They walked around the room as he introduced her to the men and their wives. Dior looked around trying to see if she saw one black person feeling out of place.

"Ms. Gibson, if you don't mind, I would love to steal Mr. Night away from you for just a moment. I want to introduce you to some very important men," the older man said.

"Are you going to be alright here by yourself?" Clyde asked leaning down to her ear.

"Yes, I will be alright. I'm going to find something to drink," she replied.

"Don't get too wasted, I plan on doing some damage tonight," he stated with a grin.

And like that, she was alone around a bunch of people she didn't know. Finding an empty table to sit at, she made herself comfortable. One of the waiters wearing an all-black suit with white gloves walked towards her with a shiny silver tray filled with champagne glasses. He stopped at her table, she took a glass off the tray, and took a sip.

"Would you like to dance?" a man asked walking up to her, he was very handsome. From his accent, it sounded like he was British.

"Um, no, that's okay."

"Are you sure?" he asked, reaching his hand out for her to take it.

Well, I was bored sitting around doing nothing."

"Alright," she finally agreed, sitting her glass down. Dior took his hand and was escorted to the dance floor. He wrapped his arms around her, lightly placing it at the middle of her back.

"What's your name?" he asked.

"Dior."

"Dior, hmm, that's an interesting name," he said with a smile.

"Thank you. I guess."

While they danced and talked, Dior was finding herself beginning to have a good time, until she looked over and made eye contact with Clyde. Her body instantly tensed up, and her dance partner looked over to where she was looking.

"Who is that?" he asked.

"My date," she answered as Clyde walked towards them. Without saying a word, he removed Dior from the Brit's grasp.

"What did I tell you?" he said in a whisper.

"I don't know, what?"

"I told you I don't like anybody touching you."

"It was just an innocent dance, Clyde."

"Yes, an innocent dance that will get someone killed. You think I'm playing?"

"No, just a little dramatic is all."

Feeling his chest muscles tense up, she looked up into his eyes and could see he was upset with her. The music finally ended, and they both made their way back over to the table. He was clearly upset with her. She could tell by the way he was looking. He was about to say something until the man at the microphone asked for everyone's attention.

"Welcome, ladies and gentleman to our annual black tie event. As everyone may know, proceeds from this evening will go to the charity that I found many years ago: PURE. I have worked many years to make life better for children in Africa that are suffering with HIV. Now, without further ado,

I will pass the mic off to Mr. Write, the Master of Ceremonies."

"Thank you, Mr. Price, we will be starting the bidding off with lot number one. Do I hear twenty-thousand dollars?"

"Twenty," a man said in the far distance.

While everyone was bidding on the first lot, Dior sat there listening to everyone bid. Clyde slowly moved into her and whispered in her ear. "I can't wait to devour you," he said. Dior didn't reply, she pretended like she wasn't phased by what he said, but in all reality, she was squirming in her skin, feeling warmth between her legs.

"Thirty thousand, sold. That's a great start for the night."

"We have lot two, two weeks stay at a luxury chalet in Zermatt, Switzerland donated from the good Mr. Clyde Night. Let's start the bidding off at twenty-thousand."

"You have property in Switzerland?" Dior asked shocked.

"Mmhm," he replied.

"Forty-thousand," a familiar voice shouted. Dior quickly turned and looked for the person that just bid, that's when she made eye contact with her sister.

"Fuck! Did you invite her?" Dior asked turning back around facing Clyde.

"No, I didn't invite her."

"Then how the hell did she get here?"

"Anyone is allowed to come as long as they have money," Clyde nonchalantly replied.

"Fifty-thousand," Dior suddenly blurted out.

"What the hell are you doing." Clyde replied

"You think I'ma let Dajah stay in one of your luxury homes?" Dior sassed.

"It's for charity," he said.

"I don't care; she's still not staying."

"Seventy-thousand!" Dajah shouted. Clyde looked over at Dior and dared her to bid.

"Where the hell she get that kinda money?" Dior questioned.

"Seventy-thousand, do we have eighty?" the man said.

"Sold to the beautiful woman in the back." Everyone started clapping, but Dior started feeling some type of way.

"Don't move."

"Whatever," Dior replied still in her feelings about the auction.

"I'm serious, Dior."

"Okay, Mr. Night," she replied sarcastically with a chuckle. He got up and walked over to another table.

Taking another sip of her champange, she took out her phone and began to scroll through Instagram.

"It's a surprise to see you here," Dajah said, sitting down beside her sister.

"Why would it be?" Dior questioned.

"Because this isn't your type of scene, being around all these wealthy people." Dior rolled her eyes already fed up with her sister's bullshit.

"What you want, Dajah?"

"Shit, I just wanted to thank you for letting me spend a few nights at your man's place."

"Its one of many, Dajah, so it's not all that serious."

"By your random bid, it seemed like it was serious."

"Well, I had to spice it up, get the most I could get out of you, and the trick seemed to work."

"Ahh, here you are, dear. I would love for you to meet someone," a stranger said.

Dior looked up to see who he was speaking to, and she realized he was speaking to Dajah. Dior couldn't help but burst out laughing. Dajah had a look of disgust.

"Shit, hoes all over the world," Dior said as she got up from her seat to walk away from her sister.

"You don't have to worry, sis, your secret is safe with me," Dior sarcastically stated before walking away from the table. As Dior walked around, she couldn't find Clyde anywhere

"It's so good to see Clyde with someone?"

"Excuse me?" Dior replied, turning to face the woman. Ahe looked older, had pale skin, blonde hair, smile lines.

"I said, it's so good to see Clyde with someone tonight. for many years, Clyde has searched for someone that could potentially save him."

'Save him from what?"

"Oh, my dear, from himself."

"And why would he need to be saved from himself?"

"There's a lot about Clyde that you don't understand. He is a powerful man, more powerful than you'll ever know, and sometimes, that power can turn into something horrible. No average woman can be with a man that is far from average."

"Are you insinuating that I'm average?"

"Well.. Yes, I am. Don't mean to be so forward, but a woman such as yourself couldn't possibly understand a man like him. No matter how hard you try, you'll never be able to stand beside him and give him what he needs."

"Well, I'm sorry to disappoint you, but Clyde is my fiancé, so I must be doing something right for him to choose."

She looked at Dior strangely and began to laugh like she told the funniest joke.

"Fiancé, I doubt that, my dear," she said as she looked down at Dior's hand. Dior looked at her finger. "I have not given it to her yet. She only deserves the best, and the best I haven't found," Clyde said, walking up behind Dior.

Dior was both startled and relieved that he showed up when he did. He reached out his hand for her to take it, placing her small hand into his, he pulled her way.

"I'm sorry about that."

"It's okay. Who was that anyway?'

"Her name is Heather. We had history back in the day. She's a little sour after all these years because I couldn't take her snobby spoiled ways anymore. Her father is one of the riches, so if I had of married her, I would be the wealthiest men in the world," Clyde explained

"And why didn't you marry her?" Dior asked.

"Because I wanted, needed something more in a wife. I've got something to show you." Taking her by the hand, he led Dior out to the balcony. It was beautiful. It overlooked Manhattan, and it was so romantic.

"Was that you accepting my proposal?" he asked, looking into her eyes. Suddenly, Dior felt tiny looking up at him. His deep gaze felt as if he was staring down into her soul.

"And if it is, Mr. Night. Are you going to accept it?"

"No."

"What?"

"No, that's not how a proposal is supposed to go. I will propose to you the right way," he replied, taking her into his arms. Dior leaned up against his hard chest. Getting up on her tiptoes, she placed her lips on his, slowly running the tip of her tongue along his lips. He grabbed hold of her wrapping his strong arms around her.

"Please don't let go, ever," Dior whispered into his lips.

"Baby, I'm never letting you go," he replied, running his finger across her bottom lip. "I will go through hell and back, and I'll walk through fire to get to you. There is nothing or no one that will keep me away from you," he softly stated.

"You ready to get out of here?" he asked.

"But the evening is still going on, and we haven't eaten?"

"We'll order room service." Looking in his eyes, she could tell that food wasn't what he was speaking of.

"There you are, Mr. Night. Dinner is about to start. Come, you and your beautiful friend."

"Thank you, Mr. Wilson, but we're going to head home. She isn't feeling too well."

"Oh, I'm so sorry to hear that, I hope it isn't anything you ate."

"No, I think I'm coming down with something."

"Okay, dear."

"I will see you in the office Monday morning, Mr. Night. We have a lot of papers to sign," he said, shaking Clyde's hand. Clyde wrapped his arm around Dior and escorted her out.

"Clyde, are you leaving so soon?" Heather asked, stopping them.

"She isn't feeling well."

"I'm sure you can have someone to take her home, and you can stay and join us for the dinner. This whole thing is probably boring to her anyway, since it's just dinner with a bunch of wealthy people there's probably a lot of things she doesn't understand." Clyde stood there; Dior could tell that this Heather was getting to him. He began to tense up, and his jaw clenched.

"Well, I suppose if you must go, then you must go," she said before walking away.

"What was that all about?" Dior asked as he led her out of the mansion

"Nothing," he replied. Walking outside, the wind was gently blowing. "What a beautiful night." Dior said as she looked up at the sky and noticed that there weren't many stars out.

"Here is Tony. Let's get going," Clyde said, knocking her out of her trance.

"How did it go?" Tony asked.

"Don't ask," Clyde replied. They both shared a laugh. Dior was just glad to get out of there.

The next morning, Dior woke up to papers lying beside her. She sat up in bed and looked over the documents. As she read it, her heart started beating fast. She rushed out of bed and threw on a large t-shirt, then rushed in search of her phone. As she looked around the hotel, she didn't see Clyde anywhere. Finding her phone, she gave him a call

*"Morning, I take it you got the documents."*

*"Yes, I did, what did you do?"*

*"You said you wanted a bar, I noticed that you had one in your book mark, so I just took it as that was the one that you wanted, so I just did what I said I was going to do: paid for it and whatever else it needs."*

*"I didn't think you were going to do it so soon, Clyde."*

*"I'm a businessman, Bubbles. When I say I'm going to do something, I'm going to do it. I don't wait around. I didn't become a billionaire by waiting around."*

*"Well, thank you Mr. Night. You have no idea how much this means to me. I don't know how I will ever repay you."*

*"Just being beautiful and belonging to me is enough. I left you some papers that need to be signed. I need you to sign them before I make it home, so I can fax them tonight."*

She just loved it when he talked business; it just did something to her.

*"Okay, Mr. Night."*

*"And stop calling me Mr. Night."*

Dior couldn't help but to laugh.

*"I need to get back to work; I will talk to you when I get home. Also, before you leave the hotel, you have a day at the spa, and you can also do a little shopping before you return home."*

After saying their goodbyes, they hung up the phone. Dior spent an hour carefully reading over the documents before she signed her name on the dotted line.

# 17

# JOZUA

*L*ying on the massage table as one of the hoes ran her small, soft hands up and down Jozua's shaft, he was in love with the way she stroked his dick. The hoes must have had a P.H.D in stroking and sucking dick. Since Dajah had been away, he'd found himself spending majority of his time in this spot called *Happy Ending*,--it was a privately owned business that was locked out in the country. It was a good four-hour drive, but once you arrived, the drive was well worth it. Whatever you wanted, they provided. Being greeted with a glass of brandy and a white robe, the only rule they had was you must undress at the door and provide test results.

After Jozua nutted in the woman's hand, he got up from the massage table, got dressed paid for his service, and walked out. He got into his car. Deciding not to drive off right away, he sat there and checked his phone. He had gotten a few text messages while he was getting pleasured. While responding to the text message, he saw a car pulling up beside him. Not paying them any mind, he continued responding to the text message. He quickly looked up to glance at the person going inside the building. He did a double take, recognizing the person walking in. Damn, that's Dior's nigga, he mumbled to himself. Feeling some type of way about it, he rushed outta his car and stormed over to where Clyde was standing.

"What the fuck you doin' here? Do ya' girl know you here?" Jozua questioned fuming.

"I think you should be asking yourself that question," Clyde calmly stated ignoring Jozua

"I think this is something Dior needs to know about. If I'm not mistaken, she isn't the type to be with a man knowing he loves to indulge himself in a little taboo play."

"Mind your business. Mr. Adams, I assure you, you have no idea what you're getting yourself into," Clyde replied, as he felt the urge to snap Jozua's neck.

"I'm sure I know exactly what is going on here, and soon, Dior will know as well." And before Jozua knew it, Clyde had his hand around Jozua's neck lifting him up to where he was only standing on his tippy toes. "I promise you, the day you tell Dior what you saw here is the day you'll take your last breath." Clyde harshly stated loosening his grip from around Jozua's neck.

Jozua took in deep breaths as he cowardly rushed to his car and started up the engine taking off. *Shit, that nigga is nuts, I gotta tell Dior,* he thought to himself as he quickly drove away. He knew for a fact that Dior wasn't the type of woman that would want to be with a man that bought pussy especially when he had some good pussy at home waiting for him, but on the other hand, he loved his good for nothing life and didn't want to die any time soon, so instead, he decided on keeping his mouth shut for now.

## 18

---

## DIOR

*Ayy shorty, take me for the pain like a drug in my blood, and ever since I seen his face, I've never felt so in lov.e Just wanna hug, wanna kiss, wanna give you my love 'Cause you the only one I miss, baby, can you pull up? Take a flight, then we pop out on the island The Louis flip-flops or Givenchys, know we stylin-'* bianca bonnie- take me away

Dior danced around the lavish kitchen as she slid her chocolate cookies into the oven. Waking up that morning, she was in the mood to bake her some cookies, strawberry cheesecake, and a red velvet cake. Although she wasn't going to eat it all, she decided to give some of the goodies to Tony, the driver, to take home to his grand kids. She was beginning to get used to being alone so much. Since the business party, Dior hadn't seen much of Clyde, the only time she would see him was passing by when he was leaving out of his office and out the house. She checked the time on the phone and realized that her phone was dying.

Where the fuck is my charger, she huffed as she mumbled to herself. Then, she remembered that Clyde had her charger the other day when he couldn't find his. She always told him to leave her shit alone because he never put it back where he got it. Going downstairs to the living room, she checked all the drawers and nothing. She went to his office where he spent most of his time. Walking around to his desk opening empty drawers, she was beginning to get agitated. Huffing and puffing, she tried to open one of the top drawers to only discover that it was locked.

Why the fuck is this drawer locked? she asked herself, letting her curiosity get the best of her. She went into the kitchen to get a butter knife because everybody knows that a butter knife is the best tool. Taking the knife, she jiggled the drawer until it popped open. There was nothing in the drawer but a wad of money, passport, and an old pocket watch that read on the back, *Until my dying day.* She put those things to the side and noticed a small, black, leather journal that was tucked to the back. Opening the journal, she found women's names with high prices and male names beside them. "Hmm," was all she said. She knew this had nothing to do with Clyde's Real Estate job.

"What have you been up to, Mr. Night?" she mumbled to herself, then her inner detective started to come out. Remembering her cookies, she rushed back to the kitchen and took out her now burnt cookies. She wasn't in the mood to bake anything else; she wanted to know what her man had been doing behind her back. Jozua was right, though; she knew nothing about Clyde, and obviously, Clyde felt some kind of way to where he felt he couldn't share with her what he was doing. Instead, he had to hide everything from her, but she refused to be blinded by whatever it was he was doing. Going back into the office, she put everything back into the drawer. Before putting the journal back, she slid her hand in the back to see if there was anything else she was missing. She felt something small. She took it out, and it was

of a pregnant African American woman; she seemed to be
very happy. It looked like they could have been somewhere
in the country; she was surrounded by tall grass, and there
were also horses and cows in the background. She wore a
beautiful, yellow sundress with a beach hat. Turning the
picture over, it read *Layla 2000*. Feeling some type of way,
she kept the picture and put the journal back where she
found it along with his other things.

Later, that night while Clyde was sound asleep, Dior quietly
got out of bed and tip toed down to his office where he left
his laptop. She quietly went over to the desk, sat down in his
large leather chair and opened the laptop. It immediately
cut on, and to her disappointment, she had to get passed the
password. She sat there for twenty minutes trying to figure
out what his password could possibly be. Then she remembered the picture that she found, Layla was the name. She
entered it, and just like that, she was in. Not letting the fact
that he had another woman's name as his password get to
her, she quickly searched through it. Dior clicked on the
first folder that said *2001-2003*. She didn't understand what
she was reading; it was just a bunch of numbers with initials
beside them. Closing that file, she opened another that read
*2015–Current.* Opening the file, it was nothing but naked
women, and it looked as though they had some sort of
branding on their bodies. Not satisfied with the information
she found, she rushed upstairs to retrieve his phone on the
nightstand beside him. Dior quietly unplugged the phone
from the charger and rushed to the bathroom, punching in
the numbers that she saw him use on multiple occasions,
and the phone was now unlocked. Going into his apps, she

downloaded an app that tracked the phone. After she was done with his phone, she put it back on the charger, but before she walked out of the bathroom, the phone went off alerting her that he had a text message.

Meeting tomorrow morning at eight. She made a mental note about the meeting in the morning. She plugged the phone back up and went back over to the side of her bed, quietly sliding back under her plush blankets.

Being jolted out of her sleep as Clyde shifted to get out of bed, pretending like she was sleeping, she listened to him as he shuffled his feet towards the bathroom. Once he was done doing his morning routine, he left the bathroom, leaving the light on. She hated it when he did that; the light always shined in her eyes. She softly let out a small grunt of annoyance. When he heard her grunt, he rushed over to the bathroom and flicked the light off, then went over to his phone, taking it off the charger to check any messages that he might have missed while he was asleep

*Fuck!* he quietly grumbled. Responding to the text message, he shut the phone off and laid it back down on the nightstand. After an hour, Clyde was ready to leave and start his day, but before he left, he gave Dior a light kiss on the cheek, trying not to wake her. She stirred and opened her eyes as if she was asleep all along.

"You leaving, already?" she questioned in a groggy tone.

"Yes, I have a few meetings that I need to attend to today, but I should be home before seven, and maybe we can spend the rest of the day together."

He kissed her again before walking out of the bedroom. A few hours had passed since Clyde left the house. She hopped out of bed, went into the bathroom, and started on her morning routine. Once she was finished, she went into the closet to find her something to wear for that day, slipping on a pair of jeans and a off the shoulder blouse with a pair of sandals. She brushes her hair up into a bun put on a little Fenty lip gloss and headed out the door. Getting into the car, she checked the app to see if the app was working, and to her surprise, it was. She sat the phone on top of her dashboard and headed towards her destination.

After an hour of driving, she finally got to where she needed to be. Parking her car four blocks from the location, she got out and walked towards the house. Jumping over a bush, she quickly ran towards the nearest window, peeping in trying to see if she could see her man. As she moved from window to window, she couldn't see anybody but a lady that looked to be the house maid--that's when she noticed Clyde walking around like he owned the fucking place. She couldn't help but to roll her eyes at the sight of him. *Meeting, huh*? she thought. As she was about to leave, heavy, large hands were now around her neck.

"Who the fuck are you?" the tall, stalky man asked, startling Dior; she knew she was in deep shit.

"I need you to come with me," he said while grabbing her by the arm to escort her inside, but Dior wasn't going without a fight. She kicked and twisted trying to loosen his grip, but her attempts failed. His grip was like a pit bull that had a taste for blood. The guard yanked her up hard enough to where she had whiplash.

"Boss, one of the hoes tried to get away. I found her peeping in the windows," the guard said through a walkie talkie.

"Bring her to me," he responded, continuing his meeting with Clyde.

"I have something very exciting that I want you to be a part of."

"I'm not really in the mood for any parties today," Clyde responded taking another sip of his brandy. The door opened, and the bodyguard walked through with a struggling Dior

"Ahh, who is this beauty?" Kelvin questioned as he stood up and walked towards the curious Dior. Her eyes darted towards a furious Clyde, but he wasn't going to show his frustrations with Dior, so instead, he sat there expressionless.

"What's your name, beautiful?" Kelvin asked, while walking towards her. She continued to look over at Clyde expecting him to say something.

"I'm his woman." She blurted out as she looked over at Clyde."

"Is it true, do you know this woman?" For a moment, Clyde didn't reply; he stayed seated contemplating on how he should handle this situation. He thought about denying Dior's claims and letting her handle her own mess, but knowing her, her mouth would get her in more trouble that could potentially get her standing in someone's corner.

"Yeah, I know her; she's just some girl I've been fucking here and there. You know how these bitches are when you give them an inch," Clyde calmly replied.

"Bitch!" Dior blurted out, feeling some type of way about what Clyde just said. Clyde gave her a look of *Keep your fucking mouth shut.*

"I wasn't your bitch last night when we were laid up together," Dior stated, ignoring his looks. Kelvin looked back and forth at Dior and Clyde as they stood there arguing. He figured out that there was more between them than what Clyde was putting on. He'd seen Dior when he was in passing, watching Clyde, but he'd never seen her up close. This had to be the woman he always kept around him.

"If you give her to me, I can promise she won't be sticking her nose into anymore of our business."

"Hm, I don't know. You know how much a nigger could go for."

"Nigger! Muthafucka, I know the fuck you not callin' nobody a nigger with your Rico Suave looking ass."

"She's feisty too, I like that." Clyde drank the rest of his brandy, placed the glass on the desk, and got up from his seat and walked over towards Dior grabbing her by the arm.

"Let me the fuck go." Dior hissed, yanking her arm out of Clyde's grip.

"Nah, you wouldn't want her; she would only cause more harm than good for the business." Everyone stood in the office waiting for Kelvin to reply. Dior had the perfect skin complexion, and was thick just how he liked his women. He wouldn't sell her; he wanted her for himself.

"Hm, I guess you're right, although I wouldn't have any problem training her. I know that once I am done with her, she would have nothing else to say, but yessir. As of right now, I don't have time for all that. Go ahead and take her. I need you back here before nine tonight; we have a special auction to do." Clyde nodded his head in agreement, yanking Dior's arm hard enough to where it felt as though her arm was out of socket.

"Ouch, you're fucking hurting me, Clyde. Let me the fuck go." She hissed as she tried to pull her arm out of his grasp.

"You should be glad that's all I'm fucking doing. Do you have any idea what the fuck you could have done in there, and any way why, the fuck were you following me?" He barked as he rushed outside towards his car. Unlocking his car door, he threw Dior inside and slammed the door shut.

"This how you treating me now? Like I'm some kind of slut."

"Yes, now shut the fuck up. You could've had us both killed, do you not realize that?"

Dior didn't respond; she turned her body to where her back was facing him. The rest of the ride home, they didn't speak to each other. He looked over at her as if he wanted to say something, but his anger, his pride wouldn't allow it. Making it home, he parked the car. Dior opened the door slammed it with so much force, the car shook. She stormed up the beautiful brick steps, opened the front door, and slammed it shut and quickly made her way up the stairs to the bedroom where she started to pack. Once Clyde got inside, he ran up stairs taking two steps at a time.

"Where the fuck do you think you're going, Dior?" Clyde questioned as he stood in the door way."

She didn't respond, she continued to pack her things.

"Stop acting like a fucking child and talk to me." Clyde hissed as he walked towards her to get her to stop packing.

"Get the hell off me. This whole relationship is a fucking joke. I know nothing about you. This whole time, I'm over here playing wifey to you while you out here doing god knows what."

"What the hell are you talking about? You know what I do for work: I own one of the most popular real-estate companies in America."

"So, who are all those women in your computer? Better yet, who the hell is Layla?" He stood there surprised that, that name came out of her mouth.

"So, you've been going through my things, I see. You've been a busy bee."

"You got damn right I've been going through your shit, that's the only way I'ma find anything out about your ass."

He gently released his grip and slowly walked out the room. Dior threw whatever she had in her hands onto the bed and followed in behind him shouting.

"That's what the fuck I thought, you're just a piece of shit, like all these other muthafuckas out here. That's all you men do is lie to get what you want. You know, everyone was right about you, especially Jozua; I should have listened to him!" she continued to shout as she fought back tears.

"He knows nothing, Dior, you know nothing. You roam around in my office playing detective and see a couple of pictures and assume you put the pieces together, but you're far from the truth. Don't you understand if I told you anything, I would be putting your life in danger."

"I don't give a fuck about all that shit, I want to know what it is you're hiding from me. Why must you hide everything from me? I'm your fucking woman! We're supposed to be honest with each other, Bonnie and Clyde type shit, but it's all good though, Clyde. You go ahead and live this lie by yourself. I'm outta here."

And just like that, Dior grabbed her belongings, and left out the house.

# 19

## CLYDE

*C*lyde sat in his dark office sipping on Jack Daniels, he struggled for many months on whether or not to come clean with Dior and let her know about his lifestyle and the reason for everything. He goes into his desk and pulled out the picture of Layla, staring at the picture memories start to flood his mind. The mistakes that he made with her he refused to make them with Dior. Making the decision to talk to her about everything, after the night was over. He gets up from his desk and goes upstairs to get ready for whatever Kelvin had planned for that night. After he was dressed he goes down stairs and leaves out the house, with Tony standing there waiting on him. "That's okay, you can go ahead and go home." Clyde said to Tony.

"Is everything okay sir?" Tony asked, he could tell how upset Clyde was, Clyde might have been able to hid his expression on his face, he was never able to hide his emotions from Tony, that was one thing Clyde hated. "Yes, everything is fine, You gone on home and enjoy the rest of your night." He said as he got into his Benz he put the key in ignition and took off. After an hour drive he was back at

Kelvins residence, parking his car he gets out and made his way inside. "Hello Mr. Night are you here for the event?" Lucinda asked.

"Yes, where is everyone?"

"They are in the study, come follow me." Clyde follows Lucinda to the study where there were already men standing around talking, it wasn't as many as he expecting but it was enough to make a big profit out of.

"Great you're here, let's get it started." Kelvin said with excitement in his eyes. Clyde stood in the back leaning up against the wall having himself another drink.

"Gentleman, I have called everyone here tonight for a very special reason, I know you all will love what I have in store." Kelvin says loudly for everyone to hear.

"Bring them out, Kelvin shouted to no one in particular, the doors open up and boys walked in. At the moment Clyde wasn't paying attention to what was going on, he was too busy drowning his sorrows into whatever he was drinking, but when the doors opened and children walked through them. His attention was now peaked. As the boys walked towards the middle of the room you could hear the mean gasp in excitement. Their eyes glazed over as lust filled them.

"I will give you men a few to pick which boy you desire, payments will be made before the fun can begin. After Kelvin finished he walked over to where Clyde was standing.

"Isn't this great, these boys will bring in billions." An excited Kelvin stated as he watched the men touch and talk to the boys.

"How old are they." Clyde asked not taking his eyes off the crowd.

"ehh, I don't know thirteen maybe fourteen. Kelvin replied nonchalantly.

Are you serious, so this is what you're doing now whoreing children."

"Look I don't like it as much as you, but with the business comes sacrifices especially if you're trying to make money."

"Im not having no parts of this Kelvin, I have a hard enough time whoring out women, but children I refuse."

"Let me remind you, your choices of who I can and cannot whore out isn't yours to make any longer, the day you signed on that dotted line 24 years ago, was the day you signed over all rights. Do I need to make a phone call to freshen your memory." I need to make a phone call to freshen your memory?" Without replying Clyde sits down his glass and walks out, going to his car he leaves heading home, selecting children wasn't part of the deal and he wanted no parts of it, as he made his way back to his house, he noticed a car was parked in his drive way looking at his watch it was twelve in the am looking closer that's when he realized that it was Dior's car, *she must of came back to pick the rest of her things.* Clyde thought to himself, everything inside of him wanted to get out and rush inside to beg for her to come back. But he knew that wasn't going to work, it never worked when she was upset. So instead he decided to stay in his car and wait for her to leave, and just visit her when she has calmed down.

# 20

# DAJAH

*D*ajah has been away from home for two month now, after the conference in Chicago, Dajah got a phone call telling her that she needed to be in New York to close a major deal. Not making plans to stay away from home longer than she anticipated, once she finished the deal in New York Night Real Estate Corporation was now doing business in New York. Night Estate was now teaming up with one of the most successful hotels in the Manhattan area. Night Estate would build a hotel and casino complex, that will bring in more than two hundred million. Dior sat in the limo dialing Clyde's number to tell him the good news, only to get his assistant.

"I'm calling to speak to Mr. Night; this is Mrs. Adams."

"Yes, Mr. Wolf isn't in office right now. Would you like for me to take a message?" The assistant asked, but without a reply, Dajah hung the phone up. She wanted to talk to Clyde not leave a message, Dajah felt that if it weren't for her his business wouldn't be doing as well as it was, so answering the phone whenever she called, she thought she deserved that much. Later that day on her way to the airport she picked up a magazine to read while on the flight back home while sitting in the limo she reads through it that's when she noticed an article with Clyde and Dior on it reading the title it read. Hottest Billionaire in Texas Is Now Taken, throwing the magazine out the window she took out her phone and began to text the guy that she was with at the Charity event; she needed some expensive TLC, setting plans to see him once she landed in Dallas.

She was excited to be home; finally, the flight back was long and tiring all Dajah wanted to do was soak in her tub and relax in her king size bed. "Jozua!" She shouted out to get no answer, she sat her things beside the door and made her way up the stairs, "Jozua, she shouted again. Hmm wonder where he could be, she said out loud. Shrugging it off she made her way straight to her master bathroom, as she ran her bath water, she was to excite not to celebrate when she accomplished, while the water was running she made a few calls for reservations in the VIP area for that Saturday night.

After her soak, Dajah was in the mood to cook a nice dinner she thought it would be nice to surprise Jozua with his favorite meal-stuffed meatloaf, potatoes, and broccoli with cheese. and washing it down with cold red Koolaid. As she was getting everything together, the doorbell rang. Whipping my hands, she sashayed over to the door, opening the door to a white girl.

"Hello, can I help you?"

"Hi, yes. I don't mean to bother you at this time, but is your brother home?"

"Brother? I'm sorry dear, but I think you have the wrong house," Dajah said about to close the door.

"Does Jozua Adams live here?"

"Yes, he does."

"Then I have the right house."

"I'm his girlfriend, and I've been trying to get in contact with him now for two months now. but he hasn't been returning my calls.

"Contact him for what? And what you mean you his girlfriend?"

"Can I come in?" Without a reply, Dajah stepped aside and let her in. She steps into the house and looks around.

"Okay, so explain to me who you are again?"

"I'm Sandra. I've been with Jozua for the past two months now, When he took me home, he said his family was coming down, and they were racist, so he needed to bring me home to protect me. Well, after I got home, I didn't hear from him again."

"And where were you guys staying for those two months?"

"Here. Jozua said he lived here, he took me out bought me things, and he even bought me a car. The only reason I came by is to tell him that we're having a baby."

"A what?" Dajah asked.

"A baby," she repeated, cupping her bulging belly. I looked down at her stomach and noticed a bump. How the hell did I miss that when I opened the door? This mother-fucker has been fucking this Becky in my house. Dajah thought to herself

"So what do you want from him?"

"I just want him to take care of his child."

"With what money, because the money he showered you with is my money? That man you been fucking in my house is a broke nigga. He ain't even got a pot to piss in."

"I can't believe this muthafucka. He not only cheated on me and fuck a bitch in my house, but he fucked a white bitch in my house!" She shouted as she began to pass back and forth nervously.

"He told me you were racist."

"Oh, so you knew about me being his wife, and you still decided to fuck him?"

Before she was able to get a word in Dajah dived towards punching her in the face pulling her by her perfectly straight hair and dragging her all over her floor.

"Please stop, I'm pregnant."

"I don't give a fuck about that. You fucked my husband, and you think you're just going to walk up in here and think you going to take everything!"

Lifting her up by the hair, she threw her across the room. As she walked towards her, Dajah was stopped by strong arms.

"What are you doing, Dajah?"

"What am I doing, nigga what are you doing? You got this bitch up in my house. You fucking this pale monkey in my shit!" she barked trying to break his grip.

"Calm the fuck down. It ain't like that."

"It ain't like what? You even got the bitch pregnant!" Dajah shouted, twisting and turning trying to break free. Losing his hold, she slipped out and leaped towards Sandra.

"Sandra, you need to leave."

"But...what about us?"

"Bitch, you need to leave now."

Before she walked out, Dajah ran after her full force. Grabbing the nearest thing she could, and chunking it and breaking it over her head. She stumbled forward and landed on her knees outside.

"Dajah, calm the fuck down. What are you trying to do, kill her and my baby?"

"So you don't deny it then, huh nigga!" she spat, as she

began to throw shit at him anything that was within arm's reach.

"Calm the fuck down Dajah so that we can talk about it."

"There's nothing for us to fucking talk about," she said huffing and puffing.

"You need to leave before I kill you," she said, collapsing on her knees.

"Baby, Dajah, let's work this out."

"There ain't shit for us to work out. Get the fuck out!" she shouted hysterically trying to hold back the wrath.

# 21

# DIOR

*I*t'd been a week since the fight between Dior and Clyde. Later that night, she went back to his house when she thought he was gone to his meeting he claimed he needed to attend. She made sure she didn't forget the money she had stashed away from when Clyde gave her money to spend on shopping. Although she was still angry with him, she also missed him. It was just too much shit that she found and still had no explanation for what it was. Dior didn't understand what he got himself into, but at that moment, she didn't care. Even though they had broken up while she was in L.A, this time, it was different. She didn't want to leave Clyde; all she wanted was for him to come clean about the shit he was in. She would have respected him more if he told her the truth rather than hiding it from her.

After cleaning out her mother's home, Dior decided she wanted to get out the house for awhile and get some fresh air, hoping that it would help to clear her mind. Jumping in the shower to wash the dirt and dust off, she slipped on her favorite jeans and a tank top, matching them with a pair of pink Puma furry slides. As she was leaving out the door, her phone rang alerting her that she had a phone call. She looked at the Caller ID and saw British's name flash across the screen. Answering the call, the only thing she could hear was loud music.

"*Hello!*" Dior yelled into the phone to get nothing back.

"*Hello!*" she yelled again.

"*Hey, girl. Ha-ha, what you up to!*" British yelled. Dior took the phone away from her ear and looked at it as though British could see her.

"*What you got goin' on over there?*" Dior questioned, feeling a bit irritated.

"*Bitch, some of the girls came over and decided they wanted to turn up tonight. Bish, you know me; I can't turn down a good turn up.*"

Dior couldn't do anything but shake her head. As long as she had known British, she had never known her to turn anything down that had to do with partying and good dick.

"*Oh, okay,*" Dior replied waiting for British to say the reason for her calling. She was about to hang up because all she was doing was talking to whoever was in the background; Dior hated that shit. Dior felt like if you called someone, there were reasons for it, so whatever the reason may have been, say it and end the conversation; don't call a person just to talk to whoever it was in the background. That just burned her up when muthafuckas did shit like that.

"*Shit. I didn't want nothin'; I was checking on my girl. I haven't spoken to you in a while,*" British eventually stated before hanging up the phone. The call ended, and Dior was relieved, stuffing her phone back inside her purse.

*Knock! Knock!*

"The day I decide to go out is the day folks wanna bother

me," she mumbled to herself as she dragged her feet to the door. Without asking who it was, she opened it. Jozua stood there with a smug look on his face.

"What do you want, Jozua?"

"I was passing by and saw your car in the driveway and thought to come by to see how you're doing."

"You just so happen to be randomly driving by my mother's house?"

"Yea, I was in the area for this meeting and just out of the blue decided to drive by."

"Oh, whatever, so what do you want, Jozua? I ain't got the time right now to talk."

"So, you don't have time to chill and talk to ya' boy?"

"Hell naw."

"Look Dior, I know I fucked up, and I apologized numerous times, and I don't know what else I can do or say at this moment. I want us to get to a place where we can have a mature conversation and be good friends if nothing else."

Dior's mean mug was now softening up as she stood there listening to Jozua plead for her friendship back.

"You know all you had to do was tell me you were married. Granted, you didn't know that your wife was my sister. I mean, I hardly ever talked about my sister nor did I have pictures of her around my house, so I'll give you that, that you didn't know, but you knew you were married, and that's what hurt me the most. I felt betrayed by you, Jozua."

"I know, and I'm so sorry that I hurt you like that. Believe me, I wanted to tell you, and to be honest, I had plans on divorcing her when I came here to Dallas and going back a free man. But things kind of went left when you showed up; I didn't know what to do."

"So you were prepared to divorce Dajah for me?"

"For you and myself, things between Dajah and I ain't what it used to be. Shit, it ain't never been good, she only married me for looks.

"If that's the case then why you propose to her?" Dior questioned

"Haha, I ain't never proposed to that girl, she proposed to me."

"That's so typical of her," Dior replied

"Maybe that's why she was with someone else at the event, I went to in New York?"

"She was with someone and what event?"

"It was some black-tie event for charity that Clyde dragged me to, and I ran into Dajah when she was hugged all up on this white older man."

"Ahh, I see." Is all Jozua said as he stood in the doorway, Dior could tell that Jozua was disappointed in the information that she given him she suddenly felt sorry for telling him.

"I..I'm sorry I shouldn't have said anything, why don't you come in," Dior offered standing aside for Jozua to step in.

"You all dressed up where are you heading to?" Jozua asked while stepping in the house

"I don't know I just needed to get out the house and get some fresh air, clear my mind."

"Is everything alright with you and ya nigga?"

"Ehh, not at this moment, we got into a little fight the other day, and I decided to leave, I'm tired of people lying to me and shit."

"Word, you want to talk about it?"

"Not really, would you like anything to drink?"

"Sure what you got." Jozua asked as he made his way into the living room to have himself a seat." After Dior made her way back to the living room with drinks in her hands, she walked over to a waiting Jozua and handed him a cold beer.

"So what's up? How you been holding up since your mothers passing?"

"I've been doing the best that I can some days are better than others."

"Yea, I hear ya, I never had the chance of knowing my mom, when I was one she died.

"Oh wow I never knew that I am so sorry."

"It's alright, I had a good childhood nothing crazy."

"So you gonna get back with him?" Jozua asked.

"I don't know; he lied to me when all he had to do was come to me, what is it about me that people feel like they cant come to me about things."

"It's not about not being able to go to you, it's about being fearful of losing you, do you know how special you are, you're a gem very rare." Dior found herself blushing as Jozua complemented her.

"Thank you, that means a lot to me," Dior replied with a small smile.

"I think Clyde is selling women." Dior blurts out randomly, catching Jozua off guard. Jozua didn't know what to say he just sat there stunned about what just came out of her mouth.

"Okay, and what made you come to that conclusion?"

"I found some images of women on his computer; they were all naked and branded."

"Hmm, is all Jozua said."

"Hold up, you mean to tell me that he's a pimp?"

"Yes." Dior agreed.

"That shit is wild," and suddenly he had the urge to tell Dior what he saw that day at the massage parlor.

"ahem, well um I got something to tell you."

"What Jozua?"

"The other day, I was at this place and when I was leaving I saw Clyde walking in."

"What place?"

"Um..it was a massage parlor."

"A massage parlor, and what is that?" Dior questioned.

"It's a place where women preform special type of massages.

"Is that right, and you're just now telling me this."

"Yea well when I saw him I confronted him about it, told him that I was going to tell you that he's seeking pleasure else where, he then went ape shit crazy and attacked me."

"What were you doing at a massage parlor?" Dior questioned.

"Yea it is, huh? Nobody knows about it in fear of him losing everything, so please don't tell anybody.

"Yea, I won't.. I promise," Jozua swore, as he began to move in closer to her, wrapping his arms around her.

"Everything will be okay, I got you, and I will always have your back no matter what."

"Thanks, Jozua. That means so much to me," She replied. Then suddenly out of nowhere, he kisses her deeply, It was a kiss that she has never gotten from him. It has so much power, so much passion behind it, Dior wanted to fight him, but she quickly changed her mind as memories' started to flood back in, she embraced it with open arms. He spreads her legs apart so that he could slide between them. As their tongues danced, Jozua was suddenly yanked and thrown across the room. Dior frantically looks up, to an irate Clyde. His gorgeous blue eyes were now dark, and sinister his jaw hardens as he walks over to Jozua picking him up by the neck and squeezes his hands as if he was about to crush him with his bare hands.

"What the fuck Clyde, how the fuck did you get in here?"

"I had a key made," Clyde replied with his hands still wrapped around Jozua's neck. Jozua began to gasp as he tried to catch his breath,

"You had a key made to my mothers home?" Dior said as she frantically runs over towards a fuming Clyde trying to get him off Jozua.

"Stop Clyde you're going to kill him."

"That's the point," Clyde responded as he looked over to Dior, and quickly loosens his grip when he sees the fear in her eyes. Jozua clasps to the floor wrapping his hands around his neck as he coughs and sucks in as much air as he could.

"I can't fucking believe you, Clyde Dior cried out as she rushes towards Jozua's kneeling down trying to help him. An angry Clyde yanks her up by the arm and takes her upstairs to one of the spare bedrooms

"did you think I was joking when I said you're going nowhere, Dior? I came by to try to explain things to you, and you got your lips on this man— Dajah's husband." Without responding, she yanks her arm from Clyde's grip and walks towards the window, looking out it. He stood next to the door not budging.

"What the fuck are you doing with him?"

"He came by to see how I was doing after our break up," she answered in a shaky tone. He just threw Jozua across that room like he weighed nothing, Dior thought to herself.

"And you so happen to lock lips with him. Do you have any idea how mad you're driving me Dior? Argh!" he roared, pacing back and forth like a madman.

"You're going to drive me batshit crazy. Is that what you want Dior?" he growls.

"No," she replied in a soft, but shaky tone.

"You seem not to grasp the concept that seeing another man touching you drives me insane, so insane to where I want to rip his hands off his body. My life revolves around you. I can't sleep, eat, or work. I can't do shit when you are away from me. My world is upside down when you're not around me, my body aches for you when you're not near me, when you're not touching me." Closing his eyes, he runs his hands through his dark hair, trying to calm himself down.

"You know you're so beautiful, your chocolate skin, your lips, those hips, your beautiful hair— everything, I crave you, You belong to me, I am the only man that can touch you. If I ever catch another with their hands on you, I will kill him." She continued to stand there facing the window as he spoke those words. Making her heart bleed, turning to face him she slowly walks over towards him looking up at him she sees how much rage, and passion he had in them, almost to where he was deranged.

"No matter how far apart we are from each other you are mine. When I'm at work, all I think about is you. When I lay with you at night, I have to touch and smell you just so that I can sleep, Do you understand?"

"This shit you got going on with this man ends tonight."

"Nothing is going on with us Clyde," she replied in a soft tone.

"Its hard to fucking tell," he responded. He went to the door and swung it open to see Jozua standing there.

"Why are you still here? I thought you would have gotten the hint that you are not welcomed here?" Clyde harshly stated.

"This is Dior's home, not yours, so I'm staying for her not you."

Clyde was about to charge at him until Dior grabbed him by his large arms stopping him from hurting Jozua again.

"I will talk to you later Jozua thank you," She spoke quietly.

"Really Dior, like that?"

"Yes like that!" Clyde roared.

"Now, I would suggest you leave before things get really nasty." Clyde barked, puffing out his chest like a caveman. Dior has never seen Clyde this way. He's always been the calm type able to control himself and his temper. Jozua glanced at Dior with a look that sent chills down her spine and walked out the door. When Jozua left, Clyde turned facing her. Picking her up from the waist, wrapping her legs around him, he carries her back to the bedroom and throws her on the bed.

# 22

# DIOR

*D*ior cuddled up against Clyde listening to him breathing. She slowly ran her hands up and down his stomach, and in that moment, she felt complete.

"Clyde," she said quietly.

"Hmm," he answered with his eyes closed.

"We still need to talk about what happened."

"Now?"

"Yes, now," she said in a stern tone. He sat up in bed, and the only thing she could see were his eyes sparkling in the moonlight. He was so gorgeous that all she could think about was straddling his massive dick and riding him until the sun came up.

"This isn't easy for me, you know."

"What isn't?"

"Apologizing."

"Make it easy," she answered forcefully. He sat there for a moment going over what he wanted to say to her.

"I'm sorry," he finally said. "When I was younger in my early twenties, I got myself into some mess which I didn't know at the time would be hard getting out of. The woman that you saw in the picture, Layla, was a prostitute that I became possessive over. I had the men that touched her killed. Back then, I didn't give a fuck about anyone but myself and my needs. I was so focused on myself that I neglected the person that needed me the most, but when I found out that she was pregnant with my child, I wanted her out the business, and I was willing to do whatever it took to get her out, even if it cost me my life. I was ready to die for her and my unborn. I knew that pimps like Kelvin just don't let their women free without a price."

"What did you do?"

"I had to sign my soul over to the devil in order to set her free. I'm not proud of it, but it's what I had to do."

"Do you still see her?"

"No, I'm not allowed to see her or my child. I'm not allowed to get in contact with her nor ask about her. If I for any reason decided to get in contact with her, it would cost her and my child their lives."

"It is something that I will have to live with for the rest of my life," Clyde said sounding pessimistic. Dior sat there as she listened to Clyde open up about his past. A part of her was angry at the fact that there was another woman out there that bore his child. There was a woman out there that could still possibly hold a piece of his heart.

"So, where is she now? Do you know?"

"Yes, she's somewhere in Italy."

"You said you had to sell your soul, what did you mean by that?"

"I control all of the east, west, and south coast sex trafficking trade; I have to buy and sell women. I have to host these business parties and collect the money. People go through me before they get to Kelvin. The only person that answers to him is me, so if anything goes wrong, it's my neck on the line."

"And, how long do you have to do that?"

"Until my last breath. Kelvin is the man that you met that day when you decided to be nosey. He's who I answer to; he's the one who has me by the balls. I know that you're angry or even disappointed. I am not who you thought I was--this man that has everything figured out because I don't. Every day I get up and try to figure out what I'm going to do about this shit I got myself into, but in reality, there isn't shit I can do, and not coming clean with you about all of this is something that weighed heavily on my heart. Believe me, I didn't want to hide this part of my life from you, I was just afraid of losing you. I'm truly sorry, but I also would understand if you didn't want shit else to do with me."

"I'm not angry with you, Clyde, and I sure as hell ain't leaving you. I'm hurt more than anything that you would hide this from me; you said I mean everything to you, but yet, you hid the most important thing that's going on in your life from me--you having a love child, and having that child taken away from you. Things like that you share with the person you love. I understand, shit, I've done things that I've regretted, and that bitch Kelvin only has you by the balls because you allow it. Outta all these years that I've been with you, I ain't never known you to take shit from no one, and I don't understand why you're taking shit from this man. You basically run this shit, and you gave your money to some nigga that don't do shit but sit on his ass all day and bark orders."

"You don't understand, Bubbles. It's so easy for you to say all that, but when he's holding someone captive that you care deeply about, it isn't much you can do."

"Then get her. You said you knew where she is. She's in Italy, correct? Then find her address and get her before he kills her, then kill him before he kills you."

"And how would you suggest I do all this?"

"I don't know; I was hoping you had that figured out."

Clyde looked down at Dior with pride. He never had someone like her that was willing to go through it all with him and not judge his past."

"What?" she said

"Nothing. If I had known you would have reacted this way, I would have told you a long time ago."

"You're my Clyde, and I'm your Bonnie; we stick together no matter what and kill niggas who stand in our way, and you bet not forget that."

"Ha-ha."

He couldn't help but to laugh at her getting hype.

"You know, the first time I saw you, I knew I had to have you. There was something special about you that I needed and wanted in my life besides your beauty and your smile. The years that I've spent with you have changed me. To be honest, this business that I'm in, I don't want any parts of it anymore, I want out and to live my life, but here's something else," he said with his head down."

"What is it?"

"I'm leaving to go to Russia. Before leaving, I wanted to come and explain everything to you. I didn't want to leave with this hanging over our heads."

"When are you leaving?"

"Tonight," he responded, looking at his watch. "Matter of fact, I need to leave now," he said.

Getting up from the bed, he began to get dressed. Dior couldn't help but to stare at his pale, white, tight ass. If she were a painter, she would paint just his ass. Once he got dressed, he went over to her side of the bed and kneeled down in front of her.

"I will be back. If you want, you can go to my house, and we will talk about this more when I get back."

"No, I think I'm going to stay here, at my mom's home."

"Speaking of your mother's home, have you thought about what you wanted to do with it, because you know you can't live in both places?"

"Who said I can't?"

"Dior…"

"I know. I don't know, I was thinking about turning it into a woman's shelter or something of that nature."

"That sounds good; we'll talk about it some more when I get back."

He kissed her once more before walking out of the bedroom

Feeling a presence in her bedroom, Dior quickly woke up; she could feel the hairs on her arm and the back of her neck stand up. Fear rapidly ran through her body. Afraid to move, she examined the room with her eyes, and that's when she noticed a shadow standing in the dark corner.

"Clyde?" she said with a shiver in her voice.

All she could see was their shadow. Whoever it was began walking towards her slowly. She laid in bed watching them, telling her body to jump out of bed, but she was too fearful to move.

*Fucking move, Dior; don't just lay the fuck there,* she coached herself. With a swift move, she kicked the covers off her and rushed out of bed. She grabbed the lamp that was sitting on the nightstand beside her bed and threw it at her invader, hitting him over the head. He grunted in shock and fell, landing on her bed. That was her queue to run out the bedroom and get down the stairs. Before she could make it to the staircase, he leapt towards her. Knocking her down, they both stumbled down the stairs.

He was a big nigga about six-four, three-hundred pounds. She couldn't make out who he was due to him having a mask over his face. Once they landed at the bottom of the steps, he fell on top of her, and they both groaned in pain. Wrapping his large hands around her neck and squeezing until she couldn't breathe, Dior grabbed hold of his hands trying to pry them from around her neck, but he was too strong for her.

She reached up and started clawing at his eyeballs, trying to pop them out of the socket.

"Argh!" He cried out in agony, taking his hand from around her neck, but she proceeded to claw at his eyes as she kicked and twisted, trying to get him off her. Her intruder began to punch her in the face with so much force and power, that he broke her nose and knocked a tooth lose, but that didn't stop her from fighting for her life. She started screaming for her life.

"Shut the fuck up!" he shouted, putting his hand over her mouth not expecting her to bite a chunk of flesh out of his hand.

"You bitch!" he shouted, getting off her. Grabbing her by the hair, he started swinging her around like a rag doll. Throwing her across the room, she hit the wall and landed on a glass table.

"Who are you?" she murmured as pain flowed through her body like hot lava. Without answering her, he walked over to her, breathing heavily, picked her up, and threw her again across the room; this time, knocking her out cold.

Once he realized that she was passed out, he made his way to the kitchen to get himself a drink of water. He took out his phone and dialed a number.

*"Speak to me."*

*"I got her, boss,"* he said, hanging up the phone. He washed the glass that he just used and put it back where he got it. He picked up Dior like she weighed nothing and carried her out to his car.

∼

### Clyde

Finally landing in Moscow, Russia, Clyde was ready to get it over with so he could get back to Dior and begin fixing their relationship. He refused to allow her to just up and walk away from him again. It was refreshing to him to hear her say that she wasn't going anywhere.

After a two-hour drive, Clyde and Gabino, one of Kelvin's men, arrived at the mansion which sat in the middle of nowhere. Once they parked the car, they got out and began to walk towards the mansion. Going inside, there were other men who stood around mingling.

"Are you ready?" Gabino asked.

"Yep, ready to get this over with."

"Good, the auction will start soon. It's being held in this room," Gabino stated.

They walked into the room where they met up with other men who were sitting in a circle, while smoking a cigar and some drinking the most expensive liquor. Also, amongst the men were women, but not just any women; they were the madams of the night. The only time the women showed up was when there was something unique happening, so he knew there were going to either be virgins or young girls there.

"If everyone is ready, we will begin," the auctioneer stated. "Tonight, we have twenty women and a lovely treat for you, gents and ladies. Without further ado, let's begin."

And like that, the doors opened up, and a very pale woman walked out. She wore a short, black, strapless mini dress; she had beautiful, long legs and short, blonde hair. He noticed that there was a tracker around her ankle.

"She is a white female, nineteen-years-old, blonde hair, weighs one-hundred-and-nineteen pounds. We will start the bid at five-hundred-thousand!" the auctioneer shouted.

All the older men began to yell their bids. The bid ended at thirty-thousand--an older fat white man won the bid. Clyde stood there watching the men bid on the women like they were auctioning precious items. Then that's when he saw her, a beautiful, young thing. She was tall with fair skin and red hair; he knew Kelvin loved a woman with red hair.

"She's used up, so the bid will start at six thousand."

"Thirty thousand!" Clyde shouted into the crowd. The men all gasped in surprise, turning their heads in the direction of Clyde. He was no stranger and was also very well known amongst the community.

"Thirty thousand dollars going once, going twice, sold to the man in the back."

The men stood around and mumbled as they looked in his direction. At the end of the night, he spent one-hundred-thousand, buying only three women.

"Okay, men and women, now for the best part. We have a few special surprises tonight that I think you all will love. Bring the first one out. This here is Ginger, a beautiful Indian girl. She's eighteen-years-old, very exotic looking, and the best part is, she's still a virgin. The bid will start at one-hundred-thousand."

The men continued shouting their bids as Clyde stood there pondering on if he wanted to bid.

"What are you waiting for, bid on her," Gabino said as he stood next to Clyde. "One million!" he shouted. The men gasped in disbelief.

"One million dollars going once, going twice…"

"Five million," another shouted, but this time, it was the voice of a female.

All the men instantly turned their heads to see who bid against Clyde.

"Seven million," Clyde bid again.

"Seven million, folks, do we have eight?"

"Ten million dollars," the lady shouted again without taking her eyes off Clyde.

He stood there for a few thinking if he should continue. Instead, he bowed his head, letting them know that he was out. "Ten million dollars, sold to the lady in the back."

After the bidding of the young virgin, the back doors opened up, and in walked two young boys who looked to be the age of ten.

"You need to bid on them. Mr. Ashwood said to bid high."

"I'm not bidding on children; I thought Mr. Ashwood and I had an understanding that I'm not pimping out children. If he wants to bid on them, then he needs to come down here and bid himself." Clyde harshly stated, turned, and calmly walked out the room with Gabino close on his heel.

"You need to get back in there and fucking bid on those kids. Do we need to remind you about Layla? I surely don't want to call Mr…"

"Don't you ever fucking threaten me about her, or I will fucking kill you, do you understand?" Clyde seethed with clenched jaws, turning and walking away.

Making his way to the car, he didn't give a fuck what Kelvin did or said; he was standing by what he told him he wasn't doing, and that was buying children.

"Mr. Night," a female voice shouted out. "You missed such an exciting ending," the woman stated as she proceeded to walk up to him.

"No, I didn't miss anything, I came here and got what I needed, now I'm going back home."

"So sad, I was hoping that you would stay a little while longer. I would love to talk business with you tomorrow morning."

"Maybe some other time. I will be in New York some-time next week, maybe we could hook up and talk then," he said as he started walking off.

He made his way to the car about to get in until he was suddenly attacked from the back.

"Ugh," he groaned as he tumbled over. They continued to hit him in the face with the same hard object.

"Mr. Ashwood said thank you for your business, and the contract between the two of you is now void, and he will make sure to take good care of Dior," Gabino said before going into his pocket and taking out a sharp knife and stab-bing him in the stomach. Twisting the knife, he took the knife out and stuck him again on the other side.

"Argh!" Clyde grunted, falling to the ground. He laid there as Gabino stepped over him and made his way to the car and pulled off, leaving him there in the dirt to die. All he could think about was Dior and the danger she was in. He tried to get up but was in too much pain to move. Instead, he dug into his pocket in search for his phone. Taking it out, he dialed Tony's number.

"*Yes,*" Tony answered

"*I...I need help.*" Clyde spoke under a whisper. Before the phone slipped out of his hand, his mind went to the one person that no matter what, he wanted safe and happy.

*I can't die, not with Dior in danger,* he thought to himself as he started coughing up blood.

"Fuck! I'm always getting myself into fucked up situations," he mumbled.

Pressing down onto the stab wound, blood was oozing out profusely. His eyes began to cloud, and he was starting to have difficulty breathing.

Hold on Clyde, Hold on for Bubbles...

To be continued!

# ABOUT THE AUTHOR

*Ebony is an up and coming author, releasing her first, Clyde and Dior: The Richest Love. She was born and raised in Austin, Texas and has been a lover of books since she could read.*

*Battling with a learning disability, she refused to let that stop her from doing something she learned to do—writing. At the age of seven, she picked up a pencil and wrote her first short story titled One Halloween Night.*

*Ebony's life goals are to not become rich, but to be comfortable enough in life where it's suitable and perhaps own a book and coffee shop someday.*

# UNTITLED

Made in the USA
Middletown, DE
03 March 2023